RUNNING TOWARDS YOU

A BEST FRIEND'S BROTHER SECOND CHANCE ROMANCE

ANA RHODES

Stardust Publishing LLC

CONTENTS

HALEY

I tried to take in another deep, cleansing breath—they had to work at some point, right? At some point, I shouldn't want to run screaming from my own wedding.

This is ridiculous. I'm sure Marcus must be having some of the same jitters as I was having. We should talk it out and then I could walk down the aisle to him, certain of my decision.

I started for the door, having to make broad movements to account for the overly full tulle skirt of my wedding dress. This was not the dress I would have chosen for myself. In fact, most elements of the wedding were not things I would have chosen for us. But with Marcus being in the public eye as the up-and-coming star of congress, he insisted the wedding planner make all the decisions because she would know exactly what was expected of a rising politician who had aspirations for the White House.

Thus, everything was cream and beige. I still shivered at that last color and so did my best friend and maid of honor, Tess, considering she got stuck with the dowdy beige number that made her to-die-for curves look like a sack of potatoes.

"Um, excuse me. Where do you think you're going?" the wedding planner, Nadia said in a slightly shrill voice.

I couldn't wait until I no longer had to hear that voice. "I just need to have a quick word with Marcus..."

"Oh no, no, no, you can't be serious? It's bad luck for him to see you before the ceremony," she said, as if I were the stupidest person she'd ever met.

I let out a strained laugh. "That's a superstition," I started, but Nadia wasn't having it.

"That may be so, but it's been proven accurate time and time again..." she continued as my eyes darted to Tess, who was standing behind Nadia, watching me carefully.

She saw my look of panic and interceded, physically stepping in between Nadia and me. "Nadia, I'm so sorry to interrupt, but is that ice sculpture supposed to look like an angel peeing?"

"What? Oh my God, not again," Nadia huffed, grabbing a walkie-talkie from her waistband and angrily barking out orders as she hurried from the room, Tess following behind her mouthing the words 'you're welcome' as she cleared the path for my exit.

I hustled out of the bridal suite and down the hall to the opposite end of the building towards the groom's suite. Marcus was so pragmatic, his calm and no-nonsense approach to life always assured me there was a plan in place. I needed to hear his practical reasoning now before I made the biggest commitment of my life.

I knocked on the door and slowly opened it at the same time. It wasn't like Marcus and I had anything to hide from one another, and I didn't have time for manners at that moment.

"Marcus," I started, but my voice caught in my throat at the sight that met my eyes. I was staring at the back of Marcus, hunched over his trusty assistant, Skylar. He had his tux on, but his pants were down around his knees as his hips pumped furiously into a moaning Skylar.

They both stilled. Then he turned to look at me. "This is not what it looks like," he said almost instantly.

I don't know why, but I laughed. Maybe because what he said was so absurd, though it seemed to be an odd time to even note that. "I may have been born in the dark, Marcus, but I wasn't born yesterday. I can see exactly what you're doing."

There was a shuffling as he and Skylar parted and covered their necessary bits. Skylar looked between the two of us, then fled the room like a scared rabbit. I couldn't explain the feelings that were coursing through me. I should be enraged. I should be sad, but I mostly felt... numb.

I looked at him awkwardly, "I—I'll let you fix yourself up, and then we should talk," I said, turning around and closing the door behind me.

My reaction puzzled me. It wasn't like in the movies, where the woman started throwing things or dropped to her knees in agony. None of that felt like the right thing to do.

I stood outside the door, looking through the window on the opposite side of the hall unseeingly for a couple of minutes before I heard the door open behind me and Marcus cleared his throat.

"First of all," he said calmly, "I'm sorry you had to see that." And I laughed again. He said it as if I had just walked in on him masturbating, not like he'd been fucking his trashy assistant mere minutes before our wedding ceremony.

"I know it's no excuse, but I'm nervous. This is a big event, and I realize you have every right to be upset, but I just ask that..." He wavered, then forged ahead, "that we table this until after the ceremony."

I felt my mouth drop open, but he wasn't done. "Haley, we have a lot of guests waiting out there for us who have given up their precious time to see us get married. We don't want to disappoint them. I know this must have been shocking to you, but I am confident we can work through it... just not right now," he said diplomatically, as if he was talking to a political pundit.

That's when the anger finally hit in full force.

"Are you fucking kidding me?"

His eyes widened, and he looked to each end of the hall to spot any passersby. "Haley," he chastised, "lower your voice."

"The hell I will!"

He sighed as if he was dealing with a petulant child. "Haley, look, I understand you're upset, and we definitely need to have a conversation about what just happened. But you can't tell me this one little indiscretion is going to ruin everything we have worked so hard to build... or this beautiful day with all the guests who are here waiting for us at this very moment," he reasoned.

None of it made sense to me—not a damn word, and yet, I was nodding my head.

I hated to disappoint anybody, and later I would remember this moment and think I must have been in such shock that I didn't know what else to do.

I never used to be like this. I was decisive and trusted my instincts. But now, even small decisions were scary and potentially life-altering, and I often found myself second-guessing everything.

"Come on, Haley," he said. "You know I love you. My nerves got the better of me. That's all that you saw in there. It was purely physical. I could never feel the same way about her as I do about you," he said. "This is the most important day of our lives, and I know I fucked up, but please don't let it ruin everything. Let's be sensible about this."

Marcus was right about one thing. This was the most important day of our lives together, and it would not do to act rashly. Later, I would blame that reasoning as I nodded and turned to head back towards the bridal suite.

Nadia was there, directing everybody into position, and Tess was by my side.

The one thing I had insisted on was that she be the one to walk me down the aisle since my parents were gone. Nadia and Marcus both balked because it was against tradition, but I would not yield.

She'd been my best friend for most of my life, and I wanted her by my side on this important day. I stepped in stride next to Tess, and she looked at me with a worried expression. "Haley? What happened?"

I shook my head, "I... I don't quite know yet."

The other bridesmaids were heading out in front of me, half of which weren't even friends of mine but acquaintances of Marcus'. He appointed them to these positions because he thought it would curry favor for him later.

Nadia was busy barking orders as Tess grabbed my elbow and yanked me back. "Haley? If you don't want to do this, you don't have to, no questions asked."

Her gentle reminder made tears prick at the back of my eyes. Or maybe the reality of what I'd just seen hit me. I blinked them away, not wanting to mess up my makeup, and gave her a watery smile. "Thank you, Tess."

She looked at me seriously. "Don't forget the code word," she said, and I bit back a smile before Nadia snapped at us to face forward and start heading toward the alcove before the aisle.

Tess and I had met when we were twelve at our parents' respective vacation homes in Hanalei, Hawaii. We became instant friends and navigated those awkward summers as preteens and teenagers together. Anytime we got in an awkward situation or one of us wanted out because of impending embarrassment, we had a codeword. Either of us could say it, no questions asked, and the other was required to get us out of the situation. Even though it was the silliest code word we could conjure up in our twelve-year-old brains, we never changed it.

The wedding march started, and I clutched at Tess's hand. "Haley," she said in a tense whisper, "you're scaring me."

I shook my head. "Don't be silly, there's nothing to be scared of," I said as we drifted to the mouth of the aisle.

I looked down the aisle. Everybody was standing and watching me intently, smiling at the radiant bride. Little did they know I was fighting the urge to throw up.

My eyes traveled down the aisle and met Marcus', and he gave me that smile... the same smarmy smile he gave TV reporters. I'd never cared for that look, but I told myself he only did that for the camera. But now, as far as he was concerned, he was on camera, and I would only get the camera-ready version of him. No love for me or excitement over what we were about to do, no remorse for what he'd done, no acknowledgment of it at all, in fact.

I looked over at Tess, panicking, and whispered the too-long ago, pinky-promised code word to her. "Dick weasel."

She looked over at me with wide eyes. "Really?" Then she looked at the crowd, smiling.

"Yes, really. Dick weasel! Dick weasel!" I said, my voice rising.

The guests murmured quietly to one another, looking confused, and Marcus gave me a questioning look as Tess said in my ear. "Shit, Haley, I don't know how to get us out of here," before she sucked in a deep breath and said, "Fuck it! Let's run!"

Tess and I looked at each other, and then I hiked my skirt over my elbow. She grabbed my hand, and we ran out of there as fast as possible.

I registered the murmurs rising to a crescendo with the guests, the shrill voice of Nadia behind me asking me what the hell I thought I was doing. But at no time did I ever hear Marcus call for me.

We ran straight out of that church and into the waiting limo that was supposed to be whisking Marcus and me away after the ceremony to drop us off at The Lane, where we would have the reception.

Instead, the driver looked confused at me and Tess, who was still panting. "Where to, ladies?"

I looked over at Tess with raised eyebrows. "Umm..."

She shrugged, and I blurted out, "Driver, get us to the airport as quickly as you can."

That's how I ended up in the airport ticket line in a poofy wedding dress with my best friend by my side, making plans on the fly. "I'll get you some clothes at the duty-free shop. What are you going to do with this monstrosity?"

"I don't know... hock it," I added bitterly.

Tess shook her head. "I wish there was time for you to tell me what happened, but you have to promise to fill me in as soon as you land. In the meantime, after I see you off here, I'm going straight to your apartment to start packing up your things. I'll send as much as I can to Hanalei."

"I can't believe I'm doing this. I haven't been to Hanalei since before mom and dad..." I trailed off.

"I wish I could get on that plane with you," she said, but I knew that wasn't possible.

Tess was a registered nurse, and she couldn't drop everything at a moment's notice and skip town. People were counting on her. I was an elementary school art teacher, and it was summer break, so I had some time to hide away, which is what I intended to do.

I didn't want to confront Marcus, and I certainly didn't want to answer any of the reporters who wanted to know what happened between the congressional boy wonder and his runaway bride. I didn't want to hear his lame excuses about why I should forgive his indiscretion. More than that, I needed to stop and figure out why I was about to commit myself to a man who would cheat on me minutes before we were to be married, but also who I had so few feelings for.

When I looked down that aisle at him, a thought occurred to me. It should have broken my heart to see him with Skylar, but my thought was, "Well, that makes sense."

Skylar was his right hand, by his side at all times. She understood all the political gibberish he went on about and was actually interested in it. It just made sense—a lot more sense than me and him.

When it was my turn at the ticket counter, I ordered a one-way ticket to the island of Kauai. From there, I would rent a car and drive to the bungalow my parents and I stayed at every summer. The place where I had so many fond memories, and also where I experienced my biggest heartbreak—even bigger than the one I was going through now.

It didn't matter anymore, I told myself. What mattered was getting away from all this noise and my duplicitous life.

I kissed a tearful Tess goodbye and promised to call her as soon as I landed to give her all the awful details.

Then I was collecting my ticket and finding the nearest duty-free shop where I bought a pair of sweats, and an 'I love California' t-shirt. I asked the cashier for an extra big bag so I could stuff that god-awful wedding dress into it. The wedding dress was the only luggage I had, and I unceremoniously stuffed it into the overhead compartment after I boarded.

I had nothing but time to think as I made my way to Hanalei. I thought mostly about how I allowed myself to get into this situation and how I lost control over my life.

Marcus was an insensitive, cheating bastard, but I was guilty of a much bigger sin—I had given up on myself. I tamped down the real Haley, her wants and desires, and did everything in my power to mold myself into someone he wanted. I couldn't blame Marcus for that, no matter how much he got wrong.

Truth be told, I had given up on myself the moment I gave Cooper up.

COOPER

As usual, it was another gorgeous day in Hanalei.

I sighed, straddling my board and kicking my legs slowly in the water, enjoying the heat on my back. It's been slow for local tourism, and most of the visitors to the island were up the road in Princeville, so it was fairly quiet on the water this morning. Hopefully, some of those tourists would visit Hanalei so I could get a few more clients. I've been teaching people how to surf for the last couple of years and I'd just finished up with a client but decided to hang out in the water for a little while longer.

My knee had been bothering me lately, and being in the water made it feel better.

Once I was shriveled beyond recognition, I coasted to the shoreline and made my way back to my bungalow.

This stretch of beach was right behind my parents' old vacation bungalow and I'm grateful every day they bought this place because now it was mine.

The bungalows weren't as fancy as the vacation homes in Princeville, but I think that's what my folks liked about it. It was simpler and melded into the landscape.

It's not very big—only three bedrooms and no closets to speak of. Something my little sister, Tess, pitched a fit over. But she eventually got over it and fell in love with the place too.

I lived for our summers in Hanalei. And when my professional football career ended abruptly, I couldn't think of any other place I wanted to be.

I had come here to get away for a while and figure out what I wanted to do with the rest of my life. I figured I could rehab my knee by swimming every day, and figure out how I could still be a part of the sport I loved so much. But it's been two years and I'm still here—and it feels like home now.

I spent so much time on the water that several tourists asked me for surf lessons, and before I knew it, I had a fairly lucrative surfing business. After their lessons, I directed them to Mahina, the woman who has run the General Store for as long as I can remember. I wouldn't dare ask Mahina how old she was, but I remember thinking she was old when I was a kid, and she looked exactly the same now. Sometimes I wondered if she had been born an old woman.

The General Store in Hanalei had everything anyone could ever need. One side boasted a small grocery store, while the other featured sunscreen, wetsuits and surfboards and any other gear tourists might need. Mahina was delighted with the business I was sending her way, so we forged a friendly business relationship over the last few years. She would send tourists my way for surf lessons, and I would refer them back for anything else they needed while in the town.

I trudged through the sand, taking my time getting back to the bungalow. I knew by now not to push myself too hard when my knee was acting up. It made for miserable surf lessons and sleepless nights from all the aching.

I took in the scene of the bungalow. There was another bungalow next door that was connected by a carport. The second summer my family spent here, another family moved in next door, and that's how I met Haley.

I swallowed hard at the thought of her. That was the only thing I didn't like about being back in Hanalei. There were very few places I could go and not have a memory of Haley. The sight of the General Store, where we first held hands. The stretch of sandy shores where we'd first made love, the porches of our respective bungalows, where we had countless midnight talks, whispering while our parents slept, oblivious to the young love blossoming outside.

I tried to shake my head free of these thoughts. It was ridiculous. Haley and I had been a lifetime ago. We were practically children, and here I was giving in to the sweet memories of her that made me smile and ache all over. The only reason I was thinking of her more than usual was because she was getting married. If I was correct with the time difference, then she was already someone else's wife and my sister was there with her, giving her away.

My jaw clenched at the thought of her being another man's wife. That was supposed to be me before she threw it all away. I guess she got what she wanted.

I started up the steps on the back porch, heading for the little half wall that stood in between our porch and the Ellis's porch, where I hung my surfboards. As I was hanging it up, my eyes caught on something that made my heart stop.

On the other side of the wall, laid out in a lawn chair in a painfully small bikini, was a woman who made my mouth go dry. She had earbuds in and sunglasses on. And as she soaked up some sun, her hands were tapping to the music against the armrest of the lawn chair.

My eyes rolled over her smooth, tight body. She still had those long dancer's legs. She'd been in ballet when she was a little girl and I still remembered her trying to teach Tess when they were young to pirouette. Tess could never quite get it, but she wasn't the most graceful creature.

What the hell was she doing here?

My eyes continued their search, looking over her toned stomach and up to those perky breasts peeking over the cups of her tiny bikini top, and then my eye stared at her hands. There were no rings. No rings.

That's when she screamed.

HALEY

"**C**ooper! What the hell are you doing here?" I asked, sounding more shrill than I intended.

My heart was pounding a thousand miles a minute, but I couldn't take my eyes off his handsome face. There were laugh lines around his eyes as he smiled at me, but he still had that sweet lopsided grin and those hazel eyes that always seemed to see right through me. Although it wasn't all that difficult at the moment. I felt like one big, walking, open wound—anyone who looked at me could tell I was a hot mess. But the last person I wanted to see that was Cooper.

"I could ask you the same thing," he said jovially enough, although there was a slight edge in his tone. "Last I heard, you were getting hitched?"

I ripped my gaze from his, busying myself with getting up from the lawn chair and putting my cover-up on. "Yeah, uh, change of plans."

I heard him huff out a laugh behind me. "Where have I heard that before? Lord help the poor sucker who tried to tie you down," he bit out, and I stiffened.

I'd been around Cooper for all of sixty seconds and he was already bringing up the break-up—as if I didn't think about that moment every damn day of my life.

As I tightened the sash of my cover-up around my waist, I turned to face him with a determined glare. "I'm going to be staying here for a while. I hope that's not a problem."

He raised a curious eyebrow, but didn't press further. "I'll stay out of your way as long as you stay out of mine."

I nodded and stomped back into the house, shutting the door decisively behind me, then sagging against it and putting my hand over my heart, trying in vain to calm it down.

Ten years. It had been ten years since I had shared physical space with Cooper and I felt like I was a teenager all over again. What the hell was he doing here? What were the odds that he was taking a vacation at the same moment I needed to run away?

I hated the idea that I was running away, but it felt like the only thing I could do.

Once I'd landed on Kauai, I felt relieved to be here, but then I worried about how it would feel to be inside the bungalow again. It had been many years since I'd visited Hanalei, and even though I'd inherited the bungalow from my parents, I hadn't bothered to come to see it since they'd died because I thought it would be too painful. Between the memories of them—and Cooper—I didn't think I could handle it. They were taken from me so suddenly, and even after two years, it still felt like yesterday.

But when I slipped the key in the lock and took my first steps inside after so long, I felt myself smiling in relief. There were a few bittersweet moments, but mostly it felt like a safe place, especially since I didn't have to worry about bumping into Cooper. Sure, it would be difficult to deal with the memories, but it was better than dealing with the chaos going on back home.

As soon as I landed, I called Tess on the drive to Hanalei. I filled her in, in explicit detail, about what I had walked in on.

"That rat bastard. I never liked him," she had declared.

"I know, I know, but..."

"But nothing. He never realized what he had in you. Listen, I know that was probably the worst way ever to find out your fiancé was cheating, but take it as a blessing that you are free of that man."

I huffed out a sigh. "You're not wrong, but right now, I'm worried about the fallout."

I could practically feel Tess rolling her eyes over the line. "Well, you know him. He's going to spin this to his benefit somehow. And I know you don't want to get involved, Haley, but don't you dare let him spin some tale about being the jilted groom. He deserves everything that's coming to him—and worse, if you ask me. Don't be afraid to talk to the reporters and set the record straight."

Reporters. Ick.

That was the last thing I wanted to do. But it sounded like there was quite the feeding frenzy to uncover exactly what happened to the rising star congressman who was left at the altar. If I knew Marcus, by the time he was done, people would be building shrines to him, praising him for his courage in the face of heartbreak.

I rolled my eyes. It didn't really matter—I didn't care what other people thought of me. I just had to get out of there. I would stay here until the next school year started and hopefully by then there would be a hotter, more tawdry story to capture people's attention.

Regaining some of my composure, I snatched up my cell phone and dialed Tess. When she answered, I accused her, "You didn't tell me Cooper was at your parents' bungalow."

"Well, good morning to you, too," she laughed.

"Sorry," I amended. "I was just startled to see him here, that's all."

"He's doing a little more than visiting. He lives in Hanalei now," she explained.

"What? Since when?" I asked incredulously.

"Since his injury. He went out there to get away for a while, and rehab his knee, but nobody in the league was offering him any jobs, so he started a little surfing business."

"Really?" I asked in surprise. I remembered him loving the surf almost as much as he loved playing football, but I couldn't imagine him not having any connections to football anymore.

"Yeah, he doesn't like to talk about it, but not playing anymore really did a number on his head. He tells me it's peaceful there and I don't think he gets as many questions about what happened. That couldn't have been easy for him."

"Well, I can certainly understand that," I said, my shock at seeing Cooper giving way to concern.

"It doesn't bother you that he's there, right?" Tess asked after I didn't answer for a moment.

I forced out a laugh. "Why would he bother me?" I asked, hoping I didn't give myself away.

Cooper and I had been together for two mind-bendingly steamy months. But it had been a secret. Tess was traveling abroad in Europe for the summer and had no idea we got together. We knew she would have a fit, but figured we would cross that bridge when we came to it and hoped that once she realized we loved each other, she would come around. But then, when it ended so spectacularly, there was no point in telling her. No sense in hurting our relationship with her after ours didn't work.

"Besides, it's nice to know he's there in case you need anything. I mean, Hanalei is pretty safe, but it can't hurt knowing there's a big buff football dude next door in case you need backup," she said, laughing.

I groaned internally. I didn't need to be reminded of the "big, buff football dude next door." In fact, he was the last person I should be thinking about. As soon as the thought entered my head, images of a naked Cooper in the shadows of the moonlight consumed me. My face warmed with the memories of us out on the sand, him hovering over me, bringing me to one glorious release after another.

That memory made me realize how fucked up my relationship with Marcus had been. What I felt for Marcus could never compare to my feelings for Cooper. I chalked it up to a one-time phenomenon. Cooper was my unicorn. The one I sent riding off into the sunset without me.

But now I was here, and he was back.

"Haley? Are you still there, or did I lose you?"

"What? Yes, I'm still here. Sorry Tess, I'm distracted."

"I bet. I hope you're not letting that dirtbag take up too much of your brain space," she said, and even though I knew she was referring to Marcus, I couldn't help but bristle knowing I'd been reliving a sensual night with her brother.

"I'm working him out bit by bit, don't you worry," I assured her.

"Good. Make sure you get out and about too. I don't want you holed up in that house. It's not healthy," she chastised, because we both know that's exactly what I was going to do.

We talked about mundane things then and she informed me she packed up my clothes with some other essentials and would send them the next morning.

We hung up, and I puttered around the house, wandering to the window that looked out onto the porch. From my vantage point, I could see Cooper on his side of the wall, waxing his surfboard, the cords in his muscles flexing and popping. He was furiously waxing that surfboard like it had done something to him. He looked so intense and... incredibly sexy.

"Great job, Haley," I muttered to myself. "Out of the frying pan and into the fire."

COOPER

There were only so many times my surfboards need-ed to be waxed, but they were getting a hell of a working over now. Just knowing that woman was right next door... looking so goddamn good.

Of course, she would look so good after all these years, after stomping my heart into smithereens and walking away. Life's not fair.

Like taking away my football career, dropping me on this peaceful island, and then bringing her here.

I waxed my surfboards, power washed the driveway, and I have folded every piece of laundry in the house. This bungalow was the cleanest it's ever been in its life, but none of it was enough to distract me from the aching of my heart and the more persistent ache in my groin.

It was a cruel injustice to be this turned on by someone so heartless.

Finally, I couldn't take it anymore and grabbed my phone. "Tess? Why the hell is your best friend next door and not on a plane to some ritzy honeymoon resort?"

She sighed. "Why do you sound so ticked off?"

"I don't sound ticked off. I'm just... curious," I added lamely.

"Could've fooled me. Look, I don't want to get into all the details because they are hers to share. But she's had a rough few days, so take it easy on her, would you? I don't get it. You and Haley used to get along so well, but since college, you act like she's your sworn enemy."

I sighed. "That's not it. I think she got... too good for us," I admitted, hoping the truth wasn't showing through.

"Speak for yourself," she huffed. "Look, I shouldn't be telling you this, because it's none of your business, but the guy she was going to marry was not a good dude and she found out the hard way literally right before the ceremony. I'm just grateful she had the guts to get out of there when she did."

Everything in me stilled. I didn't like the sound of this. For all of my anger with Haley for what she did to us, she didn't deserve to be treated poorly. I was dying to know what happened, so I would know who I needed to hurt.

I grimaced to myself. Only Haley could still make me want to protect her after everything that happened between us.

"Cooper? Do me a favor. I know she's not your favorite person for whatever reason, but can you keep an eye on her?"

I laughed, "Keep an eye on her? Why would she need me to do that?"

"She probably doesn't. But I need you to do it for me. I wish I could've gotten away long enough to come with her and make sure she's all right, but we're short-staffed and..."

"I know Tess. You need to be at home."

"She's been put through the wringer the last couple of years. Life hasn't been easy for Haley since her parents died. I'm afraid this crap with Marcus will bring every-thing to a head."

I could hear the concern in Tess's voice and I couldn't help but feel concerned myself. Turns out there is still a piece of me that worries if Haley is okay or not.

"Yeah, I'll look after her, don't worry," I assured my little sister.

"Thanks, Cooper."

"No problem, but you know once Hanalei gets its hands on her, they'll be the ones looking after her."

She laughed, "Good, she needs that more than any-thing right now."

We said our goodbyes and hung up as I paced around the house until I couldn't take my own restlessness any-more. I marched out to the carport and grabbed a surf-board.

It would be hot out there right now, and busier than I prefer, but I needed to do something with my body other than worry about Haley, and then fantasize about all the ways I could make her forget about her troubles.

But my hope of burning off a little steam when I got in the water was short-lived.

I was bobbing on the water, staring at the same shore-line where I had taken a young Haley a dozen times.

I'd promised her the world, and I had every intention of giving it to her until she took that option away.

I wouldn't have done whatever this Marcus asshole did to her. Tess hadn't elaborated, but it was clear he didn't deserve Haley.

I tried my best to stay out of the loop when it came to the girl who broke my heart. Of course, I knew she was an art teacher at an elementary school and when her parents died in a car accident, I'd sent an anonymous bouquet of flowers. The only reason I knew she was getting married was because Tess kept going on and on about the horrible maid of honor dress she was being forced to wear. But I tried to tune out anything else I heard about what she was doing because I couldn't stand the thought of her living her life without me after all the plans we had made.

"Shit," I cursed to myself as I swam back to shore. I scooped up my surfboard and headed in the opposite direction of the bungalow towards to the General Store.

I walked inside looking for anything to distract me when Mahina called out, "What's got your panties in a bunch?"

I looked at her sharply. "Panties? What panties?"

She rolled her eyes. "Good God, Cooper, do you always have to be so literal? What's wrong with you? You look a little... tense."

"I'm just thinking," I snapped.

She raised a devious eyebrow at me. "I can see how that pains you," she said dryly. "This wouldn't have anything to do with a pretty young lady staying next door to you, would it?"

I looked away, not wanting her to observe me too closely and reveal my true feelings.

"No," I said, hoping that sounded nonchalant. "What would make you say that?"

She shrugged her shoulders. "I don't know. She came in here for a few groceries earlier, and Haley Ellis sure has grown into quite the beauty, not that she wasn't pretty before."

I rolled my eyes. Of course, Mahina remembered Haley. It was too much to ask that she wouldn't. Mahina had the memory of an elephant, and she remembered everybody who stayed here no matter how long they'd been gone.

"Really? I haven't noticed."

Mahina chuckled. "I'm sure. Poor thing."

I looked at her with a furrowed brow. "Poor thing? Really?"

She tilted her head and said in a chiding tone, "I don't know what happened between the two of you, Cooper, but you're not that mean-spirited. I don't know what's going on with that girl, but she's heartbreak walking. She tries to cover it up, but I can see it. Women my age always know."

Wanting to change the subject and needle her a bit, I asked, "And exactly what age is that, Mahina?"

"It's none of your damn business, Mr. Barclay," she said in warning, and I bit back a smile as she shook her head at me.

I grabbed a bag of chips and a couple of other junk food items and pushed them across the counter at her.

"It's slow this summer," Mahina commented.

I sighed. "I know. It's making me a little nervous."

"Me too. I promised the Mayor, I'd give him a percentage for the community center. That thing is in such disrepair the roof's about to cave in on the kids' heads. But at this rate, I won't have any profit to share."

"Don't worry, we still have the festival. That always brings in a lot of tourists. We'll make up the difference for the community center, I'm sure of it," I assured her, even though I was worried too.

Hanalei was a quaint little town. There were only a few hundred residents. We relied on tourists to keep our businesses afloat, but it had been a bit of a dry season.

"We'll drum up business somehow, don't worry," I told her.

She looked at me doubtfully and shoved me my bag of purchases across the counter to me. "I hope so. In the meantime, I'll keep praying for more tourists, while you keep pretending not to obsess over your neighbor."

I scowled. "You really are a pain in the ass."

She threw her head back and cackled as I walked away.

I strolled back to the bungalow in no particular rush, needing to get away from Mahina's teasing. Normally, I had no problem with her picking on me. It was a part of our friendly banter, but I was in no mood to hear her tease me about Haley. She had no idea the wound she was picking at when it came to Haley.

As I neared the bungalow, I heard a banging sound and the volume and rhythm accelerated the closer I got.

What on earth was Haley doing in there?

I tried to ignore it and went about my normal routine inside my house. I had the rest of the day free, since I didn't have to worry about cleaning up an already spotless house thanks to my previous efforts of trying to distract myself from the troubling woman next door.

There wasn't a surf board I owned, which was quite a few, that hadn't been waxed within an inch of its life. So I settled in to watch some baseball, which would have to do until football season started.

But it was hard to get into the game knowing she was several feet away, banging endlessly.

By the third inning, I couldn't take it anymore. "For the love of God, what the hell is she doing over there?" I muttered to myself, as I marched out of my bungalow and went next door, banging on her door. "Haley? I know you're in there, so don't try to ignore me," I called through the door.

After a prolonged moment, the door opened with her looking at me crossly.

"Why on earth are you banging on my door like that?" She asked.

I felt my lips twist into a wry smile. "Oh, you don't like that noise? You could've fooled me, because that's all I can hear next door." I spit out before I realized there were tear streaks on her face.

I sobered instantly. "Haley?"

She turned away so I couldn't see her face and ges-tured behind her. "I found all these old framed pictures my mom always meant to hang up, so I thought I would do it for her. I didn't realize I was being so loud."

I soften my stance, but I realized I'd come in pretty hot, and she avoided my eyes. "Do you want some help hanging them?" I asked.

She shook her head. "No, that's okay. I'm almost done, anyway. Sorry for the noise, I'll try to keep it down," she said, as she started to close the door.

"Haley?" I stopped her. "You know if you need anyth ing..." I trailed off because, of course, I would help her if she needed me, but saying the words somehow didn't feel quite right.

She nodded and shut the door. I felt like a grade A asshole.

In all of my upset over her being in my vicinity, I hadn't thought about how hard it was for her to be back in this place for the first time since her parents died. It was bad enough she was dealing with whatever happened with her ex. Tess said he wasn't a good guy, and while I believe my little sister, I didn't know what that meant.

I remember vividly when Tess called me to tell me Mr. and Mrs. Ellis had died in a car accident.

I thought about going to the funeral, but I didn't want to make things worse for Haley and, as mad as I still was, my heart hurt for her.

She didn't have anybody else in the world. She was an only child, and adored her parents, and naturally, she was the apple of their eyes. I couldn't imagine the world not having my little sister and I didn't want to think about the world without my parents, although I knew someday that day would come. But that someday came too soon for Haley.

I hated the sight of her banging around to cover the sound of her crying. These bungalows were close with walls like paper, and while we used to love that when we were kids because we could holler at one another through the walls, I found it wholly inconvenient now, knowing that the woman next door was struggling to keep it together. Meanwhile, I was struggling not to rush over there and pull her into my arms even though I knew that was the last thing either of us needed.

My idleness evaporated, and I decided I needed to do something. We may have started off on the wrong foot, but we were adults, and what happened between us was ancient history. There was absolutely no reason I couldn't be neighborly, especially when I knew she was going through a hard time.

I rooted around in my kitchen and was happy to see I had all the ingredients I needed. Haupia was a simple dessert, and it was an island favorite—Haley's, too.

I mixed a little water with coconut milk, sugar, and cornstarch. Now all it needed was to chill in the fridge for a couple of hours and it would be ready.

I still remembered the first time she had haupia and the way her eyes rolled back in her head when the sweet treat hit her tongue. I fell in love with everything about that facial expression and we had only been on a couple of dates at that point.

That was when I was still longing for her, the girl next door, my little sister's best friend. Tess warned me to stay away because going after her best friend would be "so gross."

But her warning came too late. I had already noticed the luscious curves Haley had grown into, and this horny teenaged boy couldn't look away. Everything she did turned me on and over the course of one summer, I had gone from tolerating my little sister's best friend to having a nose for her like a bloodhound. I could always tell she was near when I smelled the faint scent of jasmine clinging to the air.

For the last ten years, in those rare moments when I smelled jasmine again, my body immediately responded as if she were right around the corner.

"I'm a masochist, that's what it is," I said to myself as I checked the haupia to see if it was set. "No. You're just being a decent human," I had to remind myself.

This woman crushed my heart, but she'd also been through a lot recently, and she was obviously struggling. Making this dessert for her was merely a peace offering and being a good neighbor... that was it. At least that's what I told myself.

Once the dessert was ready, I threw a dish towel over the top of the fancy dish and took a deep breath, willing the nerves I was feeling to go away as I made my way to her front door and knocked, normally this time.

She opened the door, looking weary and slightly defensive, her eyes going from my face to the dish in my hands, her brow furrowed in confusion.

"I might've been a little... aggressive earlier," I admitted. "So I brought a peace offering."

Her eyes widened. She opened the door a little further, and that jasmine reached my nostrils. I inhaled deeply and willed my body to calm the fuck down.

"That's not what I think it is, is it?" she said, her delicate nostrils sniffing at the sweet treat.

I grinned at her then. I couldn't help myself. "Why don't you let me in and see for yourself?"

She stepped to the side, and I walked past her into a room that I hadn't been in for over a decade.

I'd never spent much time in the living room of this little bungalow, but there'd been more than one occasion I'd snuck in through the window of Haley's bedroom when we were younger. The vision of that room was still engrained on the back of my eyelids, considering all the memories we created there.

I moved towards the small, round kitchen table next to the kitchenette. Haley walked past me to grab a couple of bowls and spoons.

I glanced idly around the living room and saw that she had indeed been putting up some pictures. The hammer and box of nails still laid out across the coffee table.

"You didn't have to do this, Cooper."

I shrugged. "I'm man enough to admit when I've been an ass."

She laughed. "Well, that makes you one of the few then," she said, with a hint of bitterness in her tone.

"Yeah, well, I try to not get involved in business that's not mine," I said, even though everything inside of me still screamed 'she is mine, she'll always be mine.'

"You're obviously going through something to be back here."

She looked at me then. "You've been talking to your sister," she said.

"She mentioned things didn't work out with the fiancé. But she didn't tell me why."

She sighed. "Good, it's embarrassing. I don't need the entire world knowing, although I don't think that will last long."

I raised my eyebrow in question. She hastened to add, "Marcus was a public figure... a congressman. I'm just glad Tess helped me get out of there. I didn't want to face questions about why I left the congressional golden boy."

"Well shit, you should've known what you were getting yourself into... a politician? They're all self-serving ego-tistical bastards," I groused, then instantly regretted it, but she smiled softly. "Sorry. That's not what you need to hear right now."

She shook her head. "You never were one to mince words, Cooper. I wouldn't expect that to be any different now. And you're right," she said. "Hindsight is a bitch."

She left it at that and while I was dying to ask her what the son of a bitch did, it was nice to have some companionable silence as we ate our pudding. Besides, words evaded me when I saw her take that first mouthful and her eyes rolled back in her head, my dick stiffening against the fly of my jeans.

Goddammit, some things never change.

"Coop," she moaned, and I nearly came in my pants from that one syllable.

Get a hold of yourself, man.

"You always made the best haupia. I haven't had this in... well," she said, looking sheepishly at me, "a very long time." It didn't surprise me to hear she hadn't had it since we broke up. Correction: since she left me heartbroken and alone. I hadn't touched it either, much less made it.

"You were always so good at this. I wonder what else you've learned to make since then," she asked idly.

"Just that, that's the only thing I ever cared enough about to learn to make. Although I make a pretty mean grilled cheese sandwich."

She didn't answer right away, looking down into her bowl before clearing her throat and then asking, "How do you get by then? Hopefully not just takeout."

"I wouldn't call it takeout. You know we don't have much of that around here. But Mahina makes these little ready-made meals in the General Store now. They're not bad. I wish she'd lay off the pineapple, though. She puts that shit in everything."

She smiled, obviously remembering my hatred of pineapple. Mahina found it to be the perfect tenderizer for any meat, so she had a tendency to stick it in every dish she could think of.

"Yeah, it's been nice to see Mahina again, although it still boggles my mind—she looks exactly the same as when we were kids. I don't think she's aged," Haley said.

I laughed, "That's because she did her aging all at once. Mahina is eternally eighty years old. I think she was born that way."

Haley and I laughed, our heads moving close together as she looked down, biting her lip the way she always did when she was holding back a big laugh.

She put her hand down on the table and, in the process, knocked her spoon onto the floor. We both leaned down at the same time, nearly butting our heads together. "Oh, I'm so sorry," she breathed, and then we were eye to eye, only inches apart, our breaths swirling together for the first time in over a decade—it felt so right, just like it did back then.

Her eyes dilated and fell to my mouth and what little restraint I had over my cock unraveled. It surged against the fly of my pants. Blood was pumping so furiously throughout me that there was no way I was going to be able to hide my hard-on when I stood up.

But maybe I wouldn't have to.

Even as every other voice in my head was telling me this was insane, I tilted my head, my eyes falling to that luscious mouth of hers, and leaned forward.

I just wanted one more taste of her... that's when her eyes widened, and she gasped, pulling away.

Dammit.

"Cooper... I'm sorry, I..."

"No," I said, shaking my head. "That one was on me. I'm sorry, I got caught up in the moment... I should get going," I said, rising from the table and instantly regretting it as her eyes fell to my crotch.

Could this get any more humiliating? I felt like a teenage boy who'd been caught with a random, un-avoidable boner.

I cleared my throat. "Well, I have some things I need to take care of. Enjoy the dessert and let me know if you need anything," I said over my shoulder, rushing towards the door.

"Um, okay, thank you," she called after me, but I barely heard it as the door slammed behind me and I rushed back to my bungalow. I went inside my house and locked the door behind me as if I could shut out the embarrass-ment, but no, it was right there, taunting me.

What did you think was going to happen, dumbass?

She'd only been back for a couple of days. After ten years and supposedly maturing into a grown man, I had lost myself in the moment with her again. I knew better than to make a move and yet here I was, having made a colossal jackass out of myself.

I rubbed a frustrated hand over my eyes. "Not again... never again," I vowed to myself, then went to take a cold shower and pray to God I could get the image of her enjoying that first bite of haupia out of my head.

HALEY

I wanted to kiss him so badly I was still aching for it. And when Cooper Barclay stood from my kitchen table, his impressive erection straining against his pants, I felt young and desirable again. Hell, I felt downright giddy, and I couldn't say I'd felt that way since, well, since the last time I'd been with him.

I was coming to the realization that this was a Cooper thing. Apparently, I wasn't meant to have this feeling with anyone else—I certainly hadn't had it with Marcus.

I looked down at the two unfinished bowls of haupia and sighed. As delicious as it was, I washed out the bowls, the knot of remorse having ruined my appetite.

After I washed out our bowls, I headed back towards the coffee table intending to put up more pictures. But instead, I plopped down on the couch and stared at the wall, reliving the last thirty minutes... and then much further back.

For all of our talking about Mahina being eternally eighty years old, Cooper had a little of that himself, not so much in the looks department, but definitely the attitude. He could be a little grumpy and curmudgeonly, like griping about me making too much noise, and then turning around to bring me my favorite dessert, which I'm pretty sure he hasn't made since before we broke up.

I still remember the first time he made it. He had taken me out on our first official date to a fancy restaurant in Princeville. He'd been saving up to take me there, but despite all his savings, we couldn't afford much on the menu. Princeville was for wealthy tourists, not a couple of teenagers sneaking out on their first date, hoping nobody would notice them. Between the two of us, we could only afford one entrée. But I didn't care. I was on a date with Cooper Barclay, and he was staring at me like I was the only girl on earth and I was eating up every second of it.

As we were waiting for the check to arrive, one of the maître d's rolled by with a dessert cart and I spied several bowls of what I would later discover to be haupia. The little ramekins with the coconut pudding also had toasted coconut sprinkled on top, and as the smell wafted from the cart, I inhaled deeply. "Mmm, that smells good."

Ever the one to take charge, Cooper stopped the maître d' and asked him what it was. When he gave us the name, Cooper looked at me with determination. "We don't need to get that from some fancy restaurant. I can figure out how to make it for you."

I smiled at him, wondering if he would finally kiss me at the end of our date. But ever the gentleman, he'd walk me to the door and thanked me for the evening... and left me standing on the stoop. I was crushed. I thought everything had gone so well and yet no kiss.

I was fairly certain our "relationship" ended before it even started. But the next day, Cooper summoned me outside where my parents couldn't see us and presented me with a chilled bowl, a dish towel covering the top of it.

He whipped that dish towel off the bowl with a flourish and presented me with my first taste of haupia. I still remember the first bite. How sweet it was, and how it melted on my tongue. When I opened my eyes, I found Cooper staring at me intently—hunger in his eyes.

I don't know what I was expecting. I imagined our first kiss a million different ways, but I didn't expect him to grab my face and pull me towards him, slamming his mouth awkwardly across mine. But I didn't care. That was just Cooper. All surliness and passion rolled into one, his lips demanding and me loving every second of it.

That summer turned into a lot of us kissing, figuring out what worked best for us and developing our own little routine.

My walk down memory lane was interrupted by several chirps from my phone. Reception was spotty on the island, so it wasn't uncommon to get a whole cluster of messages at once when the signal connected. That's also why I was grateful my parents had kept their landline. The old cream-colored corded phone hanging on the kitchen wall was older than I was, but it was handy when cell phones failed.

The last few days had been fairly quiet, and I'd taken that as a blessing. I was sure Marcus would try to get a hold of me eventually, but I didn't know what I wanted to say to him. It seemed obvious to me we were over. What else needed to be said?

There were more than just a few messages that came through on my phone. Once it started chirping, it nearly bounced off the couch cushions with its buzzing.

I picked it up and saw headline after headline. I dared to open one of them and there, plastered across the San Diego newspaper, was a picture of me, with my big poofy dress looped over my arm as I ran down the church steps. Whoever took that shot perfectly captured my speed and look of horror as I ran away. I almost laughed. The headline read "Runaway Bride Leaves Golden Boy at the Altar."

There was headline after headline, all variations painting me out to be an ungrateful, thoughtless bride ditching the heartbroken public servant at the altar.

I rolled my eyes. I knew this was going to happen, but it still stung, especially knowing Marcus was busy screwing his aide minutes before he walked to the altar.

As I closed out the headlines, I couldn't avoid the myriad of messages that had come through. There were several text messages and missed calls from Marcus.

I sucked in a breath, swallowing past the lump of dread in my throat. Might as well rip off the Band-Aid, so I pressed play on the first message.

"Haley? Haley, where have you gone? I am worried sick about you. Please pick up, please talk to me. I want to know you're safe... I love you," Marcus said tearfully.

I almost believed him, but then the next message came through, and Marcus's voice was calm, as if he was in the middle of negotiations. "Haley," he said, more authoritatively this time. "I understand you're upset, but we went over this. You are making a big deal over nothing. I wish you would calm down and talk to me."

Click.

Next message, not so calm and reasonable. "All right, I've had enough of your games. I don't know what you're trying to play, but you're messing with the wrong man. You know I won't be made a fool of. How did you think this was going to end for you? You're just some nobody art teacher, you're nothing without me," he bit out and hung up.

I heaved out a long breath. "Boy, talking about dodging a bullet."

I can't say I was surprised by his evolving anger with each message, but it still stung. Less than seventy-two hours ago, I was ready to pledge my life to this man. Now I'm hiding away from him and the world, hoping he will just go away.

I should've put the phone away then, but as if needing to punish myself, I opened the text messages. I knew there wouldn't be any messages from Tess because if she needed to reach me, she would call the landline—which she's been doing faithfully every few hours, like I was one of her patients.

There were a few messages from concerned acquaintances. And one long message from Nadia, who let me know in no uncertain terms that she would share with the press in explicit detail what an awful Bridezilla I was and how difficult I've been to work with.

And then there were text messages from Marcus. The pleas, the requests for negotiation, and then the threats. The last one really stuck with me, because he told me I would regret making a fool out of him.

Despite all his threats, I wasn't scared. Marcus didn't understand he was dealing with a woman who had nothing to lose. My parents were gone. And I lost the love of my life long ago. I was all alone on my own little island, and even though it was uncomfortable, I wasn't sure there was anything left for him to take.

That was the strange thing about this whole situation. The dust-up with Marcus was awkward and embarrassing, but it didn't hurt the way losing Cooper did. On the one hand, it made me feel oddly invincible, but on the other, I felt anxious.

I was thirty years old, and I thought I'd be starting my life anew a few days ago, but now I felt like I had nothing.

I tried to push this overwhelming feeling to the back of my mind as I methodically went back to putting pictures up on the wall and going through the rest of my parents' things, sorting through old clothes that I could give to the homeless shelter across the island, and other things I would pack to take home. But the thought of going home made my stomach turn.

When Tess made her evening call to make sure I was okay, I relayed what was going on, and she tried to reassure me. "He's nothing but bark, Haley. Don't take him seriously. But I will tell you I am so glad you got out of that situation. You know, walking in on him nailing his aide may be the best thing that's ever happened to you."

That made me laugh, and she was right. The sound of her voice and words made me feel more stable, even if just for a little while, but as the night wore on and the darkness set, my emotions got the better of me. I needed to move and get out of this place.

I went to my room and changed into the shorts, tank top and sneakers I had picked up at one of the big box stores a couple of days before.

The beach was mostly empty—a few couples spread out, making out, but I didn't pay them any attention as I ran through the sand, enjoying the pull of it as I struggled to gain traction.

I persisted, needing the movements and all the kinetic energy to settle down, and finally, my muscles prevailed over the pull and awkward lumps and bumps of the sand, and then I was flying—content that all I could hear was the thudding of my heartbeat in my ears.

I didn't want to think or figure things out. I just wanted to move until the uneasy feeling coursing through me would dissipate.

While I enjoyed moments of peace where I didn't think and just ran, eventually, my body would adjust to the unfamiliar terrain and my mind would wander. But it wasn't Marcus's nasty voicemails or threatening text messages that consumed my thoughts. It was Cooper's hazel eyes falling to my mouth as he tilted his head slightly and moved closer to me.

My body had responded more intensely in the few seconds leading up to our near kiss than it had over the last ten years, and I didn't know what to do with that.

What kind of woman runs away from her groom only to fall into the arms of the man she left years ago?

That's what I needed to remember—I left him.

Never mind the fact that it was the last thing I wanted to do, but I thought I was doing the right thing and I knew he would never understand. I don't think he wouldn't understand it now if he knew what really happened. So that's what it's come down to... all of these well-meaning decisions made in the best interest of others. Yet here I was at midnight, running my ass off, willing the anxiety and desire away.

I ran until I couldn't feel my legs anymore and then headed back to the bungalow and fell into a heap on my bed, not even bothering to undress. This would begin my unhealthy pattern of holing up during the day, and then running until I couldn't feel at night where no one would see me... at least I thought no one saw me.

COOPER

"**I** don't know, man. I think that was a lot of improvement," Russell said as he floated on his board next to me.

The thing about running a tourist-based business that I haven't quite gotten used to is how to not be brutally honest.

Many clients wanted to be schmoozed and told they were improving, even when it was clear they were regressing.

I nodded. "Well, the important thing is that you show up for every session and have a good attitude—you're great at that, my friend. But we need to get you in the water to practice more. You're still kind of timid and there's no room for fear. You have to be one with the water."

Russell looked at me skeptically. He was a transplant from the Midwest, a former executive at some corn processing plant.

"I don't know, man. I've spent most of my life away from the open water, and now I live where I'm surrounded by it. Maybe you can show no fear, but I think it's safer to let the water know you have a healthy fear of it."

I laughed. "I can follow your thinking, but it's going to kick your ass if you're scared of it... just like anything else in life. Come on, when you had to go into those plants to make sure people were doing their jobs, did it help you to go in there all timid?"

Russell's posture straightened at this. "No, you have to go in there, large and in charge," he said, with his Midwestern twang.

"Exactly, show respect, but no fear—those two are not mutually exclusive. So before the next time I see you, I want you to come out here at least two or three times to practice, okay? My instruction is only as good as your follow-through."

Russell gave me that good old boy smile of his. "I gotta tell you, Coop, you're an excellent instructor and a good friend, but you're way too honest to be a good business owner."

I rolled my eyes at him, and then something caught my eye. In the distance, I could see Haley scurrying back into the bungalow. My eyes couldn't help but follow her every movement. Russell must have noticed my distraction and jerked his head to see what I was staring at so intensely.

"Oh, that's right, you have a new neighbor," he commented. "I've seen her at the General Store a few times, but she seems to keep herself. Have you gotten to talk to her?"

Oh yeah.

"She's not a new neighbor," I corrected. "That's the Ellis' daughter," I explained, and Russell nodded sadly.

He'd moved to Hanalei three years before, so he got to know the Ellis' for a short time before they died. "Well, it's good to see her back. Is she getting things in order to sell the bungalow?"

I looked at him sharply. It hadn't even occurred to me that Haley would ever contemplate selling it. "No, I think she's just trying to get away from her real life for a while... that's just me guessing, though," I clarified, not wanting to spread any rumors.

Russell nodded in understanding. "Well shoot, I can understand the urge. I hope she gets more involved in the community while she's here. Whatever she's running away from, this place will be sure to make her feel better," he announced with confidence, and I clapped him on the back.

"Yeah, Hanalei has a way of doing that."

Russell eyed me curiously. "Is this the same girl you used to have a little something with back in the day?" He asked conspiratorially.

I furrowed my brow at him. "How did you know about that?"

He shrugged. "Gossip gets around. I may have not been here when it happened, but people get bored and tell stories."

"Yeah, well, no one was supposed to know about that..."

Russell snorted, "Please, the entire island knows about it... except your sister as I understand it," he said looking at me, raising his eyebrow in question, "Wait? Does she still not know you and that girl were a thing?"

I glared at him and shook my head. "No, and she never will. We were kids. It was nothing, no reason to get Tess all upset."

"Mahina didn't seem to think it was nothing. She was talking about you like you were some sort of Romeo and Juliet, the island's own star-crossed lovers."

I pressed my lips together and growled out in frustration. "Mahina has the biggest mouth of anybody I've ever known."

Russell chuckled, "Well, you're right there, but boy does she have some juicy stories."

"If it's all the same to you, I would prefer if you didn't continue to spread them. Haley and I are adults now, and it's water under the bridge."

Russell eyed me skeptically. "Oh yeah? Then why are you eyeing her like you haven't eaten for days and she's your next meal?"

I straightened up on my board and gave him a warning look, which caused him to put his hands up in mock defeat.

"Remember what I said about practicing, and get out of here for God's sake," I groused. I could hear him chuckling as he paddled towards the shoreline.

I waited until he was out of sight before I directed my eyes back to Haley's bungalow. As much as it irritated me to admit it, Russell was right. I couldn't deny that I'd been watching her closely, and she was worrying the shit out of me.

Since the day we almost kissed, she's stayed penned up inside that bungalow, only darting out now and then for provisions in town. But everybody in town noticed how she kept to herself and hurried back to the house. The only time she seemed to go out freely was at midnight. Every night at midnight that girl ran the shoreline, her anxious energy wafting from the water straight to where I watched from the porch.

If someone had seen me, they would probably think I was being creepy, and maybe it was a little creepy, but mostly I was worried and that irritated me even more.

Haley had made it perfectly clear years ago that she was done with me. Then a few nights ago she'd looked horrified when I was about to kiss her. That just renewed my heartbreak. I was still nursing hurt feelings over our breakup, and she was figuring out how to not be some hot shot's wife.

Though in my gut, I knew there was more to it. Haley was never the kind of person to chase glory. In fact, it made her uncomfortable.

I signed on with an agent my junior year of college when it became apparent I would be drafted the following season. My agent, Bo, made the trip to Hanalei that fateful summer and warned her things would move quickly once I was signed to the National Football League, so she would need to be prepared. After his visit, she was openly anxious about the future and how she would fit into an NFL player's life. I promised her she would never lose me, but there was something about the new life we were facing that shook her foundat ion... or maybe that's just what I told myself to ease the heartache of being unceremoniously dumped by the love of my life.

Love of your life? Listen to yourself, you sappy jackass.

Still, I was convinced there was more to her late-night runs than whatever had gone down with this guy she was about to marry. It sounds like she dodged a bullet. The last time I spoke with Tess, she'd asked how Haley was doing and, not knowing what else to say, I was honest with her. I told her she kept to herself, not talking to anybody, and went on these late-night runs. I hated sharing details I knew she would worry about, but it was her best friend, and she deserved to know the truth.

There was a part of me that loathed to hold anything back from my sister after the enormous secret Haley and I kept from her years ago.

In a conversation we had a couple of nights before, she let her worry get the best of her and spewed out a hateful rant against Haley's ex-fiancé, Marcus. According to Tess, she'd never liked him. He was fake, controlling, and the worst part was that Haley had spent the entirety of their relationship trying to fit into his world.

I would have never asked her to do that.

"It got to where I hardly recognized her anymore, Cooper. It was awful. She was just a shell of herself. As hard as it was for her, I can't tell you how elated I was when she looked at me at the end of that aisle and said the codeword."

I laughed. "She actually used the codeword?" I asked. They'd told me about their codeword when they were twelve, and I was forbidden to know what it was, but it always made them fall into a fit of giggles, so I'm guessing it was utterly ridiculous.

"When are you going to tell me what the word is?" I'd prodded out of curiosity.

I could practically hear her stubbornness wafting through the phone line. "You'll never hear it from me. We pinky sweared."

I rolled my eyes. "And everybody knows you cannot break the most sacred of oaths—the pinkie swear," I teased.

"Exactly," she confirmed in all seriousness.

"I appreciate you looking out for her, Cooper. I'm hoping to arrange some time off soon so I can come out to be with Haley. I wouldn't mind seeing my big brother either," she added in a much lighter tone.

And though I would love to see my little sister again, there was a part of me that was immediately annoyed by the thought of her being here with me and Haley.

Except there is no you and Haley.

I felt guilty wishing Tess would stay away for a little while longer. She was the one person who Haley had left... and that's when it hit me.

These midnight runs weren't about leaving her fiancé at the altar... they were about loss.

The two people who had loved Haley more than anything in the world were gone, and if my math was correct, she started seeing Marcus shortly after they'd passed. It appears she was trying to create a family for herself, but was she desperate enough to give herself up in the process?

That was the thing about Haley. She and her folks never had that contentious relationship that most kids had with their parents growing up. The three of them genuinely seemed to be friends, and now her two biggest fans were gone.

She needed more people around her—more community and support. She needed me, and that both terrified and delighted me.

The trouble was, she had no idea how much she needed me... but she was about to find out.

Later that night, I had come to a decision, and it made me nervous as hell. A few minutes before I normally saw Haley slipping from her house for her midnight run, I knocked on the door. No answer.

"Haley?" I called out in an authoritative voice. "I know you're in there, so you might as well open up... Haley?"

I could practically feel her willing me to give up and go away, but she forgot how stubborn I could be. "Haley, if you don't open this door, you'll give me no choice but to huff and puff and blow your..."

The door flew open with an irritated Haley glaring at me.

"Cooper? What do you want?"

I didn't answer her question, just gave her a once over then said, "Change into your swimsuit. We have somewhere to be."

She looked at me like I had grown another head. "What? It's almost midnight," she argued, as if that meant anything.

"Indeed it is, and I know this is usually when you go running, but we're going to do something a little different on the beach tonight," I informed her.

Her cheeks reddened. At the thought of it, I could feel my own face heat. Haley and I spent many wild late nights on the beach. A swell of satisfaction warmed me, knowing that's where her mind went.

Not so far from the memory after all, hey Hales?

I cleared my throat, remembering the mission at hand. "I'm not taking no for an answer Haley, and will not leave you alone until you come out here in your swimsuit, so you might as well get it over with."

She gave me a dubious look. "How exciting," she said wryly.

I laughed and was relieved when she turned into the house, letting the screen door slam shut but not bothering to close the door. I smiled over my small victory, but my sense of triumph vanished when she emerged from the dark living room in a tiny bikini that left nothing to the imagination.

Good God, what did I get myself into?

"Alright then," I said, blowing out a long breath and hoping to God I could somehow mask my boner. "Grab a board, we have work to do," I said, directing her to the row of surfboards on my side of the carport.

She looked at me and muttered, "I sure hope you know what you're doing."

I offered a dark laugh, "Me too."

HALEY

I didn't know what game Cooper was up to, but I was in no mood for it.

Except Cooper doesn't play games.

The voice reminding me of that fact was annoying—and not wrong.

Cooper had never been one to play games. Forthright to a fault, he is actually the exact opposite of Marcus.

It's been a week since I'd walked out of my own wedding, and I'm realizing I don't recognize the person I was when I was with Marcus. I don't know what possessed me to stay in that relationship. He was unlike anyone I'd ever dated before and at the time, I thought that was a good thing. But now I can't help but wonder what I saw in him other than stability and somebody who was always in charge.

In this particular moment, however, he and Cooper had one thing in common: they were both bossy.

Cooper was back to his old bossy self, and I bit back a smile. I'd been a little dismayed when he interrupted the time I usually slipped from the house to go for my run, but he was determined. So at his instruction, I went and put on my bathing suit and then followed him to his side of the carport, where he selected a small board for me.

"Cooper, I have no idea how to surf," I said.

"I know you don't. That's why you're going to learn," he said, his board under his arm as he led me out across the sand.

I hurried to keep up with his long strides, struggling with the weight of the board underneath my arm. "Listen, I know this is your thing now, but do you have to convert everybody who comes to the island?"

"Of course not, but you? Yes," he said without turning around, but I could hear the smile in his voice.

"Why me?" I asked, instantly regretting it. The one thing I always cherished about Cooper was his total honesty. But sometimes he could be a little much. I didn't know if I could handle it in my current fragile state.

"Because you need to get out of that house and commune with nature. It will make you feel better," he said simply.

"I commune with nature," I protested, still struggling to keep up with him in the thick sand. "You told me yourself you saw me going out for my runs."

"Not that kind of nature," he was quick to say.

I laughed. "Oh, I'm sorry. I didn't realize there was a specific kind I needed to be taking part in," I answered sarcastically.

"There is," he said without a trace of humor. "You're out there running, letting your mind run in a million different directions, and that's not getting in touch with nature. You're here to learn something new and focus all of your concentration on it. Your mind won't be able to stray and do all the unhealthy things it's been doing."

"Since when did you become a therapist?" I asked, irritated.

He stopped then, so abruptly that I almost ran into him with my board.

"It's all about mental agility. Sometimes things happen in life that challenge us, and it's perfectly understand-able to want to hide away, but if we do that for too long, we lose our ability to cope and then we have a hard time dealing with anything... I'm not a therapist, but I had to learn that lesson the hard way. So it's time to stop feeling sorry for yourself, get out of that bungalow to learn something new and commune with people. And I know you'll appreciate the irony that this advice is coming from me, of all people."

I looked at him in mock horror, then started laugh-ing uncontrollably... because he was right. I didn't know what to do with that.

Cooper was a lot of things: marginally grumpy, forth-right to a fault, and he never required a lot of social inter-action, but even he was sensible enough to know that a human being needed some socialization to survive. And if he, as a person who had little use for most people, was telling me I needed interaction, I knew I was in trouble.

My laugh turned into a sob, and I hiccupped, choking on my cry as I turned my head away so he wouldn't see, but it was too late. He'd already heard it.

He moved closer and placed a gentle hand on my elbow. "Haley, I can't pretend to know what you've been through, but I know what a huge waste it would be if you locked yourself away from the world and how much Chuck and Diane would hate that," he said, referring to my dad and mom.

The tears started flowing freely then and for the life of me, I couldn't stop them. Cooper didn't console me and let me cry it out, even as he kept us moving towards the water. Once we reached the edge, we placed our boards atop the gentle, slow waves. We started my first surf lesson with tears streaming down my face, and I listened intently, not bothering to wipe them away.

What was the point? We both knew I was broken, and he'd already seen the ugliest parts of me and didn't seem to give one shit about it, other than to make sure that I was here, out in the world. With him.

"There you go, that's it, you're doing really well," he encouraged me as I struggled to keep my balance on the board. "Remember to breathe, Haley. Just breathe, and don't think of anything else."

I did as instructed, sucking in a deep breath through my nose and letting it out through my mouth. Little by little, my muscles relaxed, and my body didn't feel so separate from me for once.

"Okay, Haley, now open your eyes," he said.

I really didn't want to, but I did as he said and opened my eyes. I'd successfully kept my balance on a surfboard in the water, but that's not the only thing I noticed when I opened my eyes. Cooper was in front of me. The deep blue velvet of the Hawaiian night sky stretched out behind him and the water, illuminated by the near full moon, created a glow around his head. It was almost as if my grumpy ex-boyfriend had a halo around him. Who would've thought?

The breath I'd worked so hard to suck in quickly got snatched from me.

"Haley? Are you okay?" He asked with concern.

I smiled, "I think I will be," I told him honestly. He smiled, and I was reminded that he knew me better than anyone, and I would indeed be just fine.

After floating on our boards in silence for a few more minutes, he declared, "I think we should head in. I don't want to wear you out before your next session."

"When's the next lesson?" I asked, a little worried.

"Same time tomorrow," he informed me.

I cocked an eyebrow. "What if I'm busy?"

"World domination will have to wait, Haley. Surf lessons first."

That sounded about right coming from Cooper Barclay.

We walked in companionable silence back to the bungalows and put the surfboards back on their racks.

"Tomorrow we'll need to clean up those boards and wax them," he told me. How could I argue? It wasn't like I had anything planned.

He walked me to my door like a gentleman and when I turned to face him, I realized I didn't know what to do with my hands because all they wanted to do was reach for him.

He watched me intensely as I stuttered out, "I don't know what possessed you, Cooper, though I suspect your sister had something to do with it."

"Tess doesn't know anything about this, and she's not going to hear anything from me," he said solemnly, and I stilled.

He'd uttered those words once before, a very long time ago, and we both stopped, acknowledging the memory before I cleared my throat and said, "Well, whatever it was, I appreciate it. But I don't want you to feel obligated."

"No obligation. Knowing you were in there all day was quite annoying," he admitted, and I laughed.

"So sorry, my mere existence annoys you."

"You know what I mean, Haley," he said. "There's more than one way to drive a man to distraction, and you've always had my number."

I felt my mouth go dry. I was losing the battle with what to do with my hands and before I could talk myself out of it, I reached for him. What's worse—he didn't stop me. My hands cupped his face, the stubble from his unshaven jaw pricking my palms in the best way.

"Coop," the one syllable sounded like it was ripped from my throat. His eyes stay trained on mine as I leaned forward.

But when I was a hair's breadth away from touching my lips to his, his gravelly voice interrupted, "Don't do it if you're going to regret it, Haley," he warned. "I never want to be one of your regrets... not again."

I searched his eyes and the rawness I saw there ripped at my heart. Then I was closing the distance between us, not only driven by desire, but the need to put a salve on the vulnerability I'd glimpsed in his eyes.

Our mouths crashed together, and then my back was pressing against the screen door as he pushed me back, his mouth hungrily drinking from mine. He tasted like heaven and we drank it in, savoring every bit. The familiar and exciting way his tongue dueled with mine, the way he nipped at my bottom lip, making me moan against him and the way his hand clawed into my wet hair while the other clutched at my hip, bringing me closer so I could feel the undeniable hardness beneath his trunks.

Soon we were backing our way through the door, and I don't know how we made it across the dark room, but then we were on the couch, Cooper's sure, steady weight on top of me. My body was burning with desire and lust, and the overwhelming feeling of coming home.

In the years since I left Cooper, I'd been floating aimlessly, doing everything I could to find my footing, trying to find a place to land and now I was here on my parents' old couch, beneath my ex-boyfriend's hard muscular chest, the feeling of his thudding heart beneath my palm and feeling for the first time in ten years that I was safe—and home.

Cooper's hand migrated beneath the cup of my bikini top, palming my wet breast, my nipple pebbling beneath his rough palm. But my realization of just how complete this felt caused panic to surge through me.

I wasn't that twenty-year-old girl in love with the football star trying to figure out how to break it to her best friend that she'd fallen in love with the older brother who'd been declared off limits. I wasn't the woman willing to risk it all because he was my forever.

I was thirty years old, running away from my problems. I was a runaway bride, with more media coverage on me than I ever hoped to get in my lifetime, which was zero.

No matter how badly I wanted to, I couldn't go back, so the realization that Cooper felt like home struck me even harder.

Oh my God. How had I gotten it so wrong all these years?

Just because I'd gotten it wrong didn't mean I needed to mess everything up now. That would be selfish.

With a heavy heart, I pushed at his chest, breaking the kiss and he looked at me, dismayed.

He must've seen in my eyes what I was about to say because he stopped me and said, "Haley, no, please, not again."

I felt the tears slipping from my eyes, hot and wild, down my cheeks. It seemed like no matter what I did, I turned into an ugly crying mess in Cooper's presence.

"I'm sorry, Cooper. I don't want to risk... hurting you again."

His jaw tensed as he straightened and sat up on the couch, looking away from me. I sat up too, fixing my cockeyed bikini top, and watched him. After a long moment, he looked at me with a solemn expression, pain in his eyes. "It's too late for that, Haley," he said, breaking our gaze, rising from the couch, and walking quietly out the door.

I sobbed into my hands. Why do I keep putting myself in this position, watching Cooper walk away? And why do I have to be the one to break his heart every damn time?

COOPER

Just as soon as the screen door slammed behind me, I was turning on my heel. She may have rejected me again, but there was something Haley Ellis needed to understand more than anything else at that moment.

I walked back into the house without knocking. She was still on the couch, her hand on her face, sobs quietly wracking her body and it took everything in me not to drop to my knees, rip my heart out and offer it up to her. That's not what Haley needed right now. She needed some sense talked into her. When she heard me, she yanked her head up, trying to cover her face, as if I wouldn't see she'd been crying.

"Listen to me. If you don't want me, that's one thing and I'll try to understand, even though I'll think you're full of shit. But you need to hear one thing from me," I told her, hoping that my voice didn't sound as shaky as I felt. She looked up at me, and I took that as my cue to lay it out for her. "I don't want you using this as an excuse to hide away, you hear me? I don't want you using that douchebag ex of yours as an excuse to hide away either... I get the world is scary, but you don't have to face it alone, regardless of what you think. Step outside, rejoin the world—they will embrace you, I promise... you're too special for them not to."

Her eyes were wide and disbelieving. There was a prolonged silence before she said, "Easy for you to say, Cooper. You haven't known me for over a decade. I'm not the girl I once was—I haven't been her for a long time. To tell you the truth, I don't know who I am anymore. I don't recognize the girl in the mirror. I know you're trying to help, but you have no idea what I've been through. What it's like to lose everything and how hard it is to make decisions in the face of losing what little you have left."

Even though my heart was still breaking for her, a tendril of anger wrapped itself around my gut. I was the one she left behind. It was my heart she'd broken, and yet here she was talking about being the one who had lost everything. She had no idea what a life-altering catastrophe it was to lose her.

"You're right, I don't know shit, I guess. You got it all figured out, Haley. Just stay in this bungalow, tucked away from the rest of the world for the rest of your life, if that's what makes you happy. But you're being selfish by removing your light from the world. Not making a decision is a decision too," I reminded her, before I turned around and stormed out again.

Sweat was pouring down my back, and I knew I had to stink, but I didn't care. I was in the midst of pulling off the comebacks of all comebacks,

and it couldn't be at a better time. We were playing our rivals, and the showdown was so hyped, we were featured on national television as the college football Game of the Week.

It was the first game of the season and I'd convinced Haley to come see me play. It had only been a few weeks since we'd left Hanalei to go back to school.

Soon I'd be graduating and was already being scouted by several NFL teams. I would need help navigating the process to ensure I landed with a team who would value me and my contributions. That's where Bo came in. I'd interviewed several agents, but he seemed to know his stuff and have my best interest at heart.

Bo embraced my competitiveness and love of the sport—and that I wasn't interested in commercial contracts or TV spots. He understood my need for teamwork and consistency in an unpredictable sport.

So after some careful consideration, I signed him as my agent. It felt good knowing I was doing well enough that an agent would take the time to sit on the sidelines watching me when he had dozens of other clients, but I felt even better knowing my girl was out there cheering me on.

If we won the game, I wouldn't hold back my affections when the TV cameras swung to see the star quarterback. I'd swing her up in my arms and kiss her for the entire world to see and let the pieces fall where they may. Tess would be upset at first, but she would come around. She loved us both.

When I scored the game-winning touchdown, I looked out at the crowd and found Haley. She beamed at me and waved, but even from a distance, I could tell she had her sad eyes on. That's what I always called it when she was worried about something. She would start chewing her lip and her eyes would go big like one of those Precious Moments figurines.

When it came time to celebrate on the sideline, Haley wasn't there, so I didn't give my public declaration of love for her like I'd hoped. Instead, she was waiting outside the locker room, looking tense.

I went to her immediately, ignoring my teammate's claps on the back. "Haley? What's going on? Are you okay?"

She was gnawing on her bottom lip. "Cooper, I don't know how to say this," she started, but I cut in.

"Just say whatever it is baby," I encouraged and watched as her eyes held mine, swimming with unshed tears. Instinctively, I knew whatever was about to come out of her mouth would be life-changing. When she said the words, it was a such a shock that when I remember the moment, I block out the words so all I remember is her sad face and then her walking away as I stood there dumbfounded.

I don't know how long I stood there, my teammates looking at me strangely as they shuffled around me to get into the locker room. Then I felt Bo slap his hand on my back and tell me in a comforting voice, "it's probably for the best son. You've got a lot ahead of you. Remember that."

I always appreciated his words, even though I knew right then and there they weren't true. I knew I'd lost the best thing that ever happen to me. And even though I had a successful career in the NFL, the highs I got from scoring touchdowns, winning games, and talking to the fans would never reach the highs of having Haley in my arms.

These were the thoughts that kept rolling around in my head as I tossed and turned after I left Haley's place. That, and the look of utter abandonment and confusion on her face when I walked out on her.

If I were a lesser man, I would've taken some sort of enjoyment out of that, remembering how abandoned I'd felt when she left me. As it is, it was taking everything in me not to crawl back to her and beg to stay by her side even if she didn't want me and that just made me feel like a pathetic loser all over again.

I've had so much success in my life and though I've had some setbacks with my knee, all of it has felt hollow without Haley by my side. It has always amazed me how all the success in the world can be overshadowed by the absence of someone important.

When I finally fell into a fitful sleep, I dreamt I was standing at an altar, much like I imagined Haley's ex had done, waiting excitedly for her appear. Only to catch the horrified look on her face before she scooped up her skirts and hightailed it out of there.

I don't know how Marcus responded, but in my dream, I started running. There was no pain in my knee. It was as good as new and damned if I wasn't determined to catch up with her and I got close. I ran up on that frothy white veil blowing behind her, and I was mere centimeters from being able to touch her when a persistent ringing sound worked its way into my dream. It took my attention from her just long enough for her to gain speed and get away again, and I jerked awake. It took a good minute for me to realize the ringing was my phone next to my head.

It stopped, and I looked over at the clock. "What the hell?" I murmured, seeing that it was only 5:15 AM. Who was trying to call me at this hour?

I plopped my head back down on my pillow, trying to calm my racing heart. I wasn't sure if I was out of breath because the phone startled me awake or because of my disturbing dream. My knee ached as if I'd actually been running that hard after Haley.

When I looked at the phone to see who was trying to get a hold of me, I saw it was Bo. I didn't hear from him much these days. I'd been out of the game for over two years now with little prospect of going back.

He swore he was working tirelessly to scout coaching positions or consulting gigs, but nothing had come up, and I'd wondered on a few of occasions how hard he tried, although I couldn't blame him. I wasn't the hottest thing anymore—I was damaged goods. He had a hoard of up-and-coming clients who were in good physical health. It wasn't uncommon for the injured guys to be shuffled to the back of the line.

When I first got hurt, I called him nearly every day to see if there was anything new. Tess pointed out this just wound me up more, and if I wasn't careful, it would take me even longer to heal.

"Cooper, I know you don't want to hear this, but it might be time to consider a life that doesn't involve foo tball... at least not in the way it's consumed your life until now," she told me. Her words pissed me off so much, we didn't speak for a week.

But Tess still took my calls... Bo, not so much. I hated to admit she was right. There was a real possibility that football wouldn't be a part of my life anymore, and I needed to accept that. It's still something I struggle with on a daily basis, so I stopped getting excited about seeing Bo's name on my caller ID's missed calls list. I set the phone aside. If it was really important, he would call back, no big deal.

My eyelids still felt heavy. Maybe I could get a little more sleep, although that seemed unlikely after the dream I'd had. I tried closing them anyway, only to be startled back open when the phone started ringing. I grabbed it without hesitation, seeing it was Bo again.

"Hello?" I answered.

"Cooper, my man, long time no talk."

I snorted out a laugh. "I'll say."

"Oh, come on Coop, don't be like that. You know I have a lot of clients to keep up with. I'm an old man. It takes me a little bit longer than it used to," he said jovially, and the tone I used to find comforting grated on my nerves.

That line had been an excuse ever since I got hurt and while part of me understood, the other part of me resented it. He'd always promised to stay by my side through thick and thin, but now that we've hit the thin part of our relationship, it's been a little tougher to track him down.

"Besides, when you hear the offer I've secured for you, you'll forget all about it," he hinted, satisfaction lacing his words.

My ears perked up and my heart rate picked up again as well. Maybe circumstances were taking a turn for me... so why was my gut screaming in warning?

HALEY

Something strange happened after Cooper left. I sat on the couch in the dark, tears streaming down my face. The memories of the last few hours ran through my head, stalling on when I'd pushed Cooper away from me and I saw the look of utter heartbreak in his eyes. I had done it to him again.

I flipped on the table lamp next to me, deciding it was a little too dramatic to be sitting in the dark crying, but when I flipped on the light, it seemed to flip a switch in me too. No matter how much I detested what Cooper said, he wasn't wrong.

My parents wouldn't want this for me. They would be devastated if they knew I was locking myself away.

I'd spent my whole life making sure everybody else's needs were met, but maybe it was time to heed my mother's warning. She said if I didn't find time to take care of myself, nobody else would, and eventually I would put myself in a position where I couldn't help anybody because I would be too depleted.

That Cooper had been the one to tell me my parents would be disappointed with how my life was going angered me and I let that anger propel me off the couch and for the first time in a week, I started looking around me. I finally saw it all so clearly.

I was sick of these walls, of the thoughts in my head—and I was sick of myself. Most of all, I was sick of people like Cooper and Marcus, who felt the need to tell me how I should live my life.

Anger, an emotion I'd largely avoided, felt good. It warmed me from the inside and out and suddenly, after feeling rudderless, I felt like I had a new direction. I had no clue where it was taking me, but I was about to find out.

Once I had my realization, I was too excited to sleep. I took a long, luxurious bath and took my time fixing myself up for no particular reason other than wanting to look good.

By the time the sun rose, my hair had dried and fell to my shoulders in soft waves. I had on minimal makeup, and for once I didn't look like a scared raccoon despite my lack of sleep. I retired the yoga pants and ratty t-shirts in favor of a sundress I haven't worn since before I met Marcus. When the boxes Tess packed for me arrived, I'd wondered why she would pack something like that, it wasn't like I would need it.

But today, I now know Tess had packed it hoping I would get myself out of this funk. I slipped on the cotton dress with a smocked bust that hugged my curves, and

I enjoyed the feel of the loose skirt swirling around my thighs. Impulsively, I twirled around like I had when I was a girl in a new dress and laughed.

"Well, I am a girl in a practically new dress," I smiled to myself in the mirror hung on the bathroom door.

I gathered up my bag and headed out, intending to stay out much longer than the rushed trips I've been making into town as of late.

I strolled towards the main drag, where practically anything a person could need in Hanalei could be found.

For the first time since I'd arrived, I kept my head up, so I saw when people waved and smiled.

Without a destination in mind, I found myself in front of the General Store, which seemed only appropriate. Mahina's was one of the few businesses that was already open and I was grateful because otherwise, I would be wandering around town looking like a doofus.

"Good morning," Mahina called out from the back.

"Good morning," I sang back, and then I saw her head pop up from behind the counter. "Haley? You're a sight for sore eyes this morning," she said, smiling and looking at me carefully.

On a whim, I twirled for her, which made her laugh. "Yes, well, the yoga pants and t-shirts are at the dry cleaners so I had to put this thing on," I told her happily.

She grinned broadly. "Well, if you ask me, you should leave those yoga pants and t-shirts at the dry cleaners. You're too pretty to cover all that up... wait until Cooper gets a load of you in that little number."

I felt my smile tighten but informed her soundly, "I'm not dressing for anybody but myself these days."

She clapped her hands together. "Atta girl, the sooner we figure that out, the more peaceful our lives are. Now, what can I do for you today?"

I looked at her and then I looked around the store, realizing I hadn't come with a list, so I stood there waiting for inspiration to strike. "I think I can find it on my own, but if you need me, I'll be in your art supply section," I told her giving her a small wave as I headed to the opposite side of the store setting my eyes on the aisle I hadn't bothered to visit since I'd been back.

Once upon a time I'd spent a good chunk of my summer days sitting in this aisle dreaming up what I could do with the various items. Nothing was fancy—this is just a General Store, after all. But to my young, burgeoning artist self, I'd seen a world of possibility in that small section of paint, brushes and canvases.

I snatched up a basket from the end of the aisle and started shoveling everything I could find into that basket, anticipating the cash I would get for hocking my wedding dress.

I suppose if I was wise, I would save that money, but at the moment, it seemed like I was doing the best thing possible with it—purchasing the healing medicine my soul desired.

Mahina gave me a conspiratorial look when I hefted my basket, full of goodies, onto the counter.

"Looks like somebody has some plans," she said.

I shook my head, "Yeah... not really. I'm just going to throw something on that canvas and see what sticks."

For a moment, I thought she was going to reach across the counter to hug me which would've been completely out of character for her, but she resisted and told me, "You go do that, and don't let anybody tell you what it's supposed to look like."

I dropped my voice and raised my eyebrow. "Just let them try."

After I left the General Store, I wandered down to the farmer's market. It was typically bigger on the weekends, but even during the week, there were consistently half a dozen vendors.

I thought I would pick up some fruit to attempt a still life in a bowl. It was overdone sure, but it was a start. I hadn't picked up a brush in months—and cleaning up the brushes from my students didn't count.

I enjoyed being out in the early morning breeze, and it was fun to talk to the people running the stands. One woman, Evelyn, was eager to talk to someone new. "You're not from around here, are you? I would remember you. You're different," she said.

"My parents and I used to vacation here during the summers, and I needed to get away, so I came back," I explained to her.

She looked at me more carefully, then nodded sagely. "It's because of a man, isn't it?"

I looked at her sharply, but she was quick to add, "Nothing wrong with that. They're always causing trouble. We wouldn't have so many reasons to run away and go back to places of comfort if it wasn't for them."

I smiled at her. "Yeah, I suppose that's true."

I reached for some mangoes, checking for ripeness, when my phone started ringing. I groaned to myself. Why hadn't I turned the ringer is off? Better yet, why hadn't I left the damn thing at home?

Evelyn looked at me curiously. "Are you going to answer that?" She asked, and once again, I had to bite my lip to hold back a laugh. Residents in Hanalei were shameless about getting in your business, and for once in my life, I liked it.

I picked my phone out of my bag and checked the caller ID. It was Marcus. I hit the decline button and shook my head at Evelyn, "No, nobody important," I told her with a smile as I went about picking fruit, and she guided me to the best ones she had.

By the time I headed home, it was late in the afternoon. I had an armload of goodies between all of my art supplies, fruit, and other items I'd picked up along the way. I dumped it all on the kitchen table, looking at my bounty with satisfaction. Nothing like a little retail therapy to make a girl feel better.

I put away all the food, except for the fruit and then started digging through my art supplies, trying to figure out where the best light was and that's when my eyes fell on the porch.

For a moment, I contemplated not sitting out there. I would be out in the open and while I didn't care if most people saw me, I knew Cooper would see me and

I didn't feel like dealing with him today. I hadn't sorted out how I felt about last night or the things he said to me, and frankly, I didn't want to. But then I felt that familiar twinge of anger that had gotten me going this morning. I had every right to be out on that porch and I wasn't required to answer any of his questions, so he would just have to get over it.

With that determination in mind, I gathered up my art supplies and hauled them out to the small table on the porch.

The beach was filled with people, but because of the porch's positioning, I had relative privacy except for Cooper's porch, which was right next to mine.

I pushed that thought out of my head and began working. My parents had a beautiful wooden bowl that I pulled out of the cabinet and positioned the fruit in it carefully. I set it down on the old wrought-iron table, where my parents used to sit and have their morning coffee. The memory made me smile. I think they could've sat out here all day, people watching, enjoying the waves coming in, and enjoying the silence of one another.

That was something I really wanted for myself—the ability to just be silent with someone. Marcus always felt the need to fill in the silence and he could not stand being still. I should've seen that as the red flag it was...

Haley—get that man out of your head and focus on your art.

I tried to do a rough sketch with a pencil on canvas of the bowl of fruit, but it wasn't coming out the way I liked it. I sat back and sighed, frustrated. It had been a long time since I'd worked at this, so understandably, my first attempt wasn't going to be a masterpiece, I reminded myself.

I let my eyes wander to the water and my heart rate picked up when I saw a familiar figure out on his board. He appeared to be with a client, and I watched them unabashedly.

Cooper was patient and instructive—like he'd always been, and I smiled.

He was too far away to see his facial features clearly, but seeing his form out there was strangely comforting and I had a flashback to the night before, when I realized he felt like home.

I ripped my gaze from the water. This was supposed to be my time—not the time to ruminate over past loves or failed relationships. I needed to figure out how to clear my head. I stared at the blank canvas again, and then I decisively pushed away the bowl of fruit and started sketching something else, though I wasn't sure where I was going with it.

I sketched the shoreline and the clouds in the background. Then I started applying some paint.

My hands took over, and I quickly covered the canvas, blending and shading, my eyes going to the shoreline, trying to capture the right colors and shadows. I didn't know how long I sat there, but it was long enough for my knees to cramp from being in the same position for too long. I didn't stop until I saw my phone light up. While I'd turned the ringer off, I'd seen it light up a few times and Marcus's name appeared on the screen.

When it lit up again, I took it as a sign to take a break. I set my brush down and put in the passcode for my phone, quickly deleting the voicemails Marcus had left—there was no point in listening to them. But then I saw I had missed a call from a different number I didn't recognize and they had left a message. It was probably just spam, but something compelled me to click on the voicemail and listen to it.

"Miss Ellis. This is Clark Rivas from Celebrity Times. We understand you had quite an eventful day last weekend and we'd like to have a sit down to talk about it. We would make it worth your while..." I was about to delete the message when I registered the figure the man had offered and my eyes nearly bugged out of my head. I should've deleted the message, but something held me back. If it were anybody else, I'm sure they would jump at the chance to make $100,000 for an hour of their time, but there was no way I could do something like that. I detested being in the public eye, and this would put me out there front and center, spilling my secrets. No, I wanted to move on.

I set the phone down and glanced at my painting, letting out a gasp. I'd been so engrossed in the moment as I was creating that I hadn't registered what I'd painted on the canvas.

While I'd managed to capture the beautiful waves, I decided I would probably never get them just right. I did a decent job of getting the afternoon sun to hang just right in my canvas sky, but smack in the middle of that canvas was Cooper on his board, looking pensive. His face was turned away, but his muscles were sweaty and gleaming in the afternoon light.

"Well, I'll be damned," I murmured to myself.

I'd subconsciously painted the one person I was trying to avoid, but at the same time, it felt great to paint again. That paintbrush in my fingers, the smell of the paint, and the afternoon breeze caressing my bare shoulders made for the most relaxing and enchanted afternoon I'd had in a very long time.

I felt more a part of the island and less a part of the mess I'd left behind in California, and I wanted to keep feeling that way. So I picked up my phone one last time and fired off a text to Tess.

Me: Hey, I'm going to shut down this phone for a while. It's driving me nuts, but I'm okay. Call the landline if you want to talk.

Tess was quick to respond with a thumbs-up emoji and a "*talk later, promise.*"

Later, when I spoke with Tess, she was concerned until I explained, "If I'm going to truly get away from the mess at home, then I need to cut off communication. It's time to focus on what's right in front of me and figure out where I go from here... not what I should've done or what I others want me to do in the future. I'm really sick of that word, should."

"Amen, sister," Tess laughed. "I'm glad to hear you're approaching it this way, Haley. It sounds like you're on the mend now."

"I hope so. It sounds corny and maybe a little self-serving... but I missed myself," I admitted.

"That's not self-serving, that's the truth. People forget they need to love themselves as much, if not more than others do. Especially women—we're trained to put ourselves last, and that it's selfish to think of ourselves."

"Is this where you holler death to the patriarchy?" I asked, teasing.

But she wasn't laughing. "I'm serious Haley. I'm tired of everyone feeling entitled to tell me how I need to feel about myself, and you should be too. We should be able to live our lives as we want and feel how we want to feel."

"I couldn't agree more."

I spent the rest of the day following my intuition, doing whatever I felt called to do, and none of it involved hiding away. When I couldn't stand my hunger any longer, I walked into town and had dinner with myself at the local taco shack. I wondered why I hadn't done this sooner.

I was about to ask for the check when the server came over and said, "another guest sent this over for you," he said, presenting me with a small plate of sopapillas. I looked at him curiously, and he turned around, pointing behind him. Evelyn, from the fruit stand, was sitting at the bar. She waved me over, so I took my sopapillas and went to her. She was with another woman who she introduced as her wife, Natalie, and we spent the next hour laughing and talking about everything and nothing. It was nice. I even told them about why I really came to the island, unable to stop myself, and they both agreed I'd done the right thing.

"You came to the right place," Natalie said. "You know, I ran away to Hanalei because of an awful experience with a man," she said, "and ran right into Evelyn. Fate was smiling on me that day. Sometimes running away is exactly what you need—you never know when you're running home," she said and I gave a strained smile, trying to forget that word and the image of Cooper that immediately popped into my head.

It was late in the evening by the time I got home. I was tired, but feeling comfortable in my skin for the first time in a very long time—maybe even since before I left Cooper the first time.

It's disturbing to realize you haven't been comfortable in your own skin for that long. But it was time to re-discover thirty-year-old Haley—she still had plenty to offer.

I went to sleep peacefully that night, happy knowing that I was on an upward trajectory now.

I got up with the sunrise, much like my parents did when we spent summers in Hanalei. As a teenager, I'd complained about being awoken so early, but they argued it was a damn shame to miss such a beautiful sunrise. I couldn't help but think that it was their spirits rustling me awake, eager for me not to miss out on another Hanalei sunrise.

Still feeling sleepy, I brewed some coffee and sipped it slowly. I was startled when I heard a knock on the door. It was tentative, but definitely there.

I walked to the door in my pajama shorts and tank top and opened it to find an uneasy Cooper.

I swallowed hard at the sight of him. Only he could look this good so early in the morning. But before I had a chance to say anything, he started, "Regardless of what happened between us, you still need to keep up with your lessons," he said, barely looking at me, his jaw tense.

Normally, I would tell him this isn't necessary or make up some excuse to get out of it because the situation is beyond uncomfortable. But after yesterday, I decided I might be open to a little discomfort... and I might as well bring Cooper along for the ride. So I gave him a big smile and said, "Let me go get my bikini," noticing the pink that stole over his cheeks before he turned away.

"Fine. I'll be out here," he said, clearing his throat.

I bit back my smile long enough to turn around and laughed to myself as I headed to my bedroom and found my skimpiest bikini.

COOPER

Our surf lessons might've been miserable if it hadn't been because Haley was inexplicably relaxed. In fact, as the days went by, she grew more and more at ease and I was delighted with this new development. I don't know what flipped the switch, but I was hearing from more and more neighbors about what a breath of fresh air Haley was and how funny she was—both things I knew to be true, but I was surprised to hear them from complete strangers.

Haley must have decided she was done hiding away. I would see her out and about on Main Street and at various places in town, happily chatting with people, and it was like the girl who had crashed back on the island with a broken heart evaporated.

I even caught her out on the porch painting a few times, and it made my heart feel like it was going to burst.

Tess called me a couple of times to check in, and each time commented that Haley sounded a lot better. I confirmed that, from what I could tell, she was indeed much better.

"It was the strangest thing, Cooper. I thought I was losing her. It's like something flipped overnight... I wonder what happened to make it click for her?" She asked idly and I couldn't help but wonder, too. I didn't think my little speech to her the night she rejected me was enough to do it, but something happened around that time. I tried not to overthink it, but it was everywhere.

Even going into the General Store that morning after my lesson with a client, Mahina was excited to tell me that Haley was going to be "just fine."

"Oh yeah? What makes you say that?"

"Because she's in here every other day getting more art supplies. Don't you see she's creating? If she's creating, then she's healing. That's the best medicine, and on top of that, she's really talented."

I nodded in agreement, then murmured, "I hope it's enough to heal her."

Mahina stopped, and in a rare moment, got serious. "It's hard to know what's going to heal us and how long it's going to take, but it's no different than you getting up on that surfboard every day. I don't know if you'd consider yourself completely healed, Cooper, but you get up every day and work at it. That's what Haley is doing. Though if you want to help her out, encourage her to get more involved with the community."

I laughed. "What are you talking about? Every time I see her, she's talking to somebody new. She looks pretty involved to me."

Mahina waved an impatient hand at me. "I mean more than that, we have the festival coming up and we could use her help. You've been such a vital part of it the last couple of years. I can't think of a better ambassador to get her involved."

I nodded nonchalantly, even though I was secretly glad for another excuse to knock on her door later to ask her about it.

When I got home and stopped by Haley's, I was slightly alarmed when she called out, "The door's open. Come on in."

"Haley," I scolded, "I could've been anybody. Don't you lock this?"

She gave me a dry look from her place behind the kitchen counter. "You worry too much," she said. "Besides, the only person who ever shows up at my door as you... although now Evelyn and Natalie will be too, because they're coming over tonight."

"Evelyn and Natalie?"

"Yeah, Evelyn runs a fruit stand at the farmers' market, and Natalie is semi-retired. They're coming over for dinner tonight. It's going to be fun, although there will probably be a lot of girl talk, so I doubt you'd want to join us, but I can make extra if you want leftovers," she said happily, as she worked at stirring something on the counter.

All of this was so different, and I felt like I was being yanked back in time, long before Haley and I split up, when she was still light and happy.

"Here, come give this a taste. I'm not sure if it's turning out right..." she said, holding out a spoon to me. I looked at it skeptically, but then dutifully took a taste, holding her eyes as I licked at the sweet concoction. "Perfect," I said hoarsely.

A thrill of satisfaction ran through me at the way her eyes observed me and then dilated at my words. Yep, there's definitely still something there. Dammit.

But there was no way Haley was going to let anything happen. She'd made that abundantly clear, so I cleared my throat and continued, " I actually had a purpose in coming over here, not just to taste test your baked goods."

"Well, I appreciate it," she said.

"No problem, Haley. I'll taste whatever you have to sample any time," I said, not realizing how suggestive it sounded until it came out of my mouth.

Her cheeks turned pink, and she smiled, as I rushed to explain, "So Mahina asked me to recruit you to help us with the festival that's coming up."

"Is it already time for that?" She asked.

I nodded. "Yeah, and it's really important this year. I'm hopeful you've noticed that the community center is in pretty bad shape. We want to use the funds from the festival this year to fix it up, but we don't have as many volunteers as past years, so we could really use your help."

I was prepared for some pushback, but she looked at me amicably and said, "Okay, what do I need to do?"

Suddenly feeling nervous, I sucked in a deep breath and said, "Well, they're having a town council meeting tomorrow night at the town square to discuss the plans and assign roles. You could come with me and I'll introduce you to everybody you haven't met yet, and then we can figure out where your skills could make the most impact."

She nodded. "Sounds good. Let me know when we leave."

I stood stunned for a moment. No arguing, no push-back. She was ready to be a part of this community, and I had to bite back the smile that was threatening to overtake my face.

"Okay, well, sounds good," I said, backing away, smiling at her.

She smiled back. "Yep, sounds good."

I felt something hit my lower back and realized it was the knob on the door. I looked at it in surprise and then looked at her. She was fighting back a laugh. "Okay, I guess I'll see you tomorrow then."

"Okay, Cooper, see you then."

Her sweet smile was the last thing I saw before I closed the door behind me and called through the door to Haley, "make sure you actually lock the door this time."

"Okay, Cooper," she sang out, as I waited. Only when I heard the lock click and Haley holler through the door, "happy now?" did I step towards my porch, calling out behind me, "Yes, Haley... yes." And for the first time in a long time, I actually meant it.

Dinner with Evelyn and Natalie was a blast. I hadn't laughed like that in so long. They'd fawned over my paintings and I couldn't tell if they were just doing that to be nice or if they genuinely meant it, but I didn't care. They were fun and completely separate from Marcus, or anyone else in my past, for that matter.

Of course, they'd heard about my next-door neighbor. Hanalei was such a small place, no one could resist noticing the "hunky, ex-football player turned surf instructor." Those were Natalie's words, not mine, but I could hardly disagree.

"Have you thought about taking a ride on his surfboard?" Natalie asked, with a cocked eyebrow, wanting all the juicy details.

Apparently, I lack a poker face because when I didn't answer, both Evelyn and Natalie squealed, then laughed, delighted. I didn't get into all the details, but it didn't seem to matter. The history Cooper and I shared played out across my face like a movie.

Somehow, we fell down the rabbit hole of what happened between me and Cooper all those years ago, how'd we'd kept it from Tess and how I'd ended up with Marcus.

"Don't you see, my dear girl?" Evelyn chided me gently, "you chose Marcus thinking he was a safe bet because he was boring and predictable. But you never really let him in, so if things went south, you wouldn't be hurt."

I hadn't thought about it like that before, and she made a decent point. I almost married a man who was cheating on me, and yet walking in on him with someone else barely caused a sting. Sure, I was mad as hell, but once that passed, I felt a whole lot of nothing for him other than regret over wasted time.

"I can see what you're saying, and honestly, the biggest pain from my breakup with Marcus is having to dodge all these reporters wanting their scoop," I admitted.

Natalie jumped in, "Girl, I'd take every dollar they threw my way and sing like a canary."

I smiled. "I know, some of the offers are pretty tempting, but that would require having cameras on me and I can't think of anything I'd hate more."

"How in the world were you in love with a professional athlete and about to marry a politician when you can't bear the limelight?" Natalie asked.

I shrugged my shoulders. "I guess I never thought about what being with them really meant for me and my privacy."

"Well, I'm glad you've begun to move on and are making friends in town," Evelyn said. "If you're not careful, we might make you the next permanent resident of Hanalei," she teased.

"Beware of this one... always trying to recruit new people to the island," Natalie piped up.

"What? There's nothing wrong with fresh faces," Evelyn sniffed.

"You just want fresh gossip and man, you hit the gold-mine with this one!" She laughed.

"Don't say that about our new friend," Evelyn scolded her wife, but I was enjoying their interaction. They were so comfortable with one another, and I wanted that too.

"Ah, don't worry about it. I'm just happy to have some nice people to talk to, and the sordid details about the runaway bride aren't a secret. And as for Cooper..."

"That information will never leave my lips, don't you worry," Evelyn assured me. "However, if you ever decide to dip into the cookie jar, so to speak, with your hand-some neighbor, I must be the first to know," she insisted, waggling her eyebrows suggestively.

"Good God Evie, what do you want her to do, roll off him, then immediately text you?" Her wife teased.

Evelyn smiled at me mischievously. "I mean, that would be ideal."

The rest of our evening was wonderful, and I went to sleep that night with my bedroom window cracked open so I could hear the waves lapping against the shore and the warm breeze drifting between the curtains and caressing my skin. The relaxation of the night with my new friends and the sweet memory of Cooper's nervous behavior from earlier lulled me.

Tomorrow I would spend the evening with Cooper and I felt as giddy as when he and I first started dating.

Except this is not a date, Haley.

I pushed the thought aside. Right now, everything in my life was going well, and I didn't want my mind to complicate things, so for once I let it go. I did not know what the next day would bring, but for once, I wasn't going to worry ahead of time. I was going with the flow like the waves.

"Okay everyone, I think everyone is here, so gather closer so you can hear me," Mayor Kahale boomed from a small stage in the middle of the town square.

"We could hear you from the moon!" another resident called out to a smattering of laughter.

Mayor Kahale made a face, declaring, "there's always a comedian."

Cooper and I moved closer to the stage with the rest of the crowd, which also closed the distance between us, and I felt relieved. Since he'd picked me up, he'd been careful to keep a respectful distance. It was as if he was afraid if he got too close, he'd catch fire.

I'd thrown on another swishy sundress and spent way too much time on my hair and makeup, but when I'd opened the door for Cooper, I caught his pupils dilate, and knew the effort was well worth it. Then his jaw hardened, and he announced we better get going before we were late.

I kept watching him from the corner of my eye as we walked through town, making small talk and asking him questions about various things that caught my eye.

Eventually, I couldn't take it anymore. "Cooper? Is everything okay?"

He jerked his head, reluctantly looking at me. "Sure, why do you ask?"

I eyed him suspiciously. "Okay, I guess we'll pretend you don't look like you're about to blow a fuse."

"What are you talking about? I don't look like I could blow a fuse. I look perfectly normal," he defended in his typically grumpy demeanor and I held in a laugh.

"Okay," I sang, "but your perfectly normal looks like you haven't been to the bathroom in a while."

He whipped his head around, eyebrows up. "Oh, you think you're funny?" he asked, trying to be serious, but I could see him struggle to keep the corner of his mouth from quirking upward.

He relaxed somewhat after that and drifted closer, but not close enough for my liking until the mayor's booming voice sounded and we gathered around the stage with everyone else. The familiar scent of salt water and Cooper's cologne assailed my senses, and I inhaled deeply, letting the familiar smell swirl inside of me, providing both comfort and excitement.

"Okay folks, first I want to thank everyone for coming out. I see some new faces out there, so that's encouraging. I'm confident we can make this year's Aloha Festival better than ever," Mayor Kahale said to a round of excited applause.

"Now, we have our work cut out for us this year. As most of you know, our community center needs a lot of repairs and this tourist season hasn't been as busy as what we've experienced in previous years, so this festival is our Hail Mary. But I know we are capable, so with the help of my trusty assistant here, Ms. Mahina, we will assign roles to your strengths, and if you aren't sure what those are, Mahina has a sixth sense for figuring that out. Once roles have been assigned, we'll split into groups and get to work! Let's do this for Hanalei!"

The crowd cheered and started talking amongst themselves as Mahina's small but sturdy form worked efficiently through the crowd with her clipboard, barking out assignments like a drill instructor.

I watched with amusement and leaned in close to Cooper to ask, "should I be worried about what you've gotten me into?"

He gave me a mischievous smile. "Now come Haley, do you really think I'd lead you astray?" The teasing in his voice warmed me. For a moment, he'd forgotten he was keeping his distance from me. Did he feel like he needed to protect himself from me?

Before I could answer his question, Mahina appeared before us. "Alright, you two lovebirds," she started and any ease Cooper was feeling disappeared. He tensed up, giving Mahina a warning look, but she took his demeanor as a challenge—no surprise there. "I hate to break the two of you up, but I need you both for very different tasks. Cooper, can you spearhead the building of the booths again this year?"

"On it," he said, "am I rounding up the same people as last time?" he asked, sounding all official, and I couldn't help but smile. As a natural leader, this was right up Cooper's alley. It was a huge part of what made him such an effective quarterback in the league. He knew when to lead and when to step back and let others shine.

"Sounds good to me," Mahina said. "Now you," she said turning to me, "I have big plans for you," she said smiling and I glanced over at Cooper in worry but he just smiled as Mahina wrapped her fingers around my elbow and dragged me across the square to a group of children jumping and talking excitedly. "Children! This is Ms. Haley. Say hi."

A scatter of "hi" and "hellos" came from children ranging in age from six to fourteen.

Mahina smiled at me, then explained. "These kids will paint a mural on the back of the grandstand and you will show them how... it needs to be done in the next few days," she added as if it was an afterthought and I shouldn't be concerned. My eyes widened as I examined the large space she was pointing to and the half a dozen children that stood before us. They all looked at me expectantly and for a moment I considered telling Mahina she was out of her mind but then a little boy only six or seven years old said, "we got this, right?"

Something kicked over in my head. I'd accomplished some hard things as of late, so why was I worried about something that came naturally to me? I smiled down at the little boy. "Yeah, we got this!" I assured him, along with the other kids.

"You all listen to Ms. Haley and come up with a game plan. Whatever supplies you need, let me know and I will provide them from the store," Mahina said before moving on to the next group, leaving me with the smiling, eager faces.

The art teacher in me took over, and I started by learning everyone's names then asking, "Okay kids, what ideas do we have for the mural? Maybe something that represents Hanalei?"

They began spewing out ideas about what represented the town to them and within a few minutes, I had the seed of an idea. An older girl loaned me her notebook and pencil, so I plopped down in the middle of the town square with the children surrounding me and sketched out a combination of our ideas.

It felt good to be in my professional element in the place that was feeling more and more like home. Coming to Hanalei started as an escape but now that I was surrounded by these kids who were so full of ideas and eager to help their community, I began to wonder what it would be like if I stayed—to become a part of this community that welcomed me with open arms.

As the kids and I were discussing the elements of the mural, I got this prickly sensation on the back of my neck as if someone was watching me. I glanced up to find Cooper across the square. He was clearly in an instructional mode as he discussed building the booths with people in his group, but his eyes were on me looking molten and possessive.

I suppressed a shiver, remembering a time, a million years ago, when I would catch him looking at me like that... and what would usually follow. *Damn.* My determination to not give into him was weakening beneath that gaze.

I tore my eyes away, forcing myself to focus on the kids and the task at hand.

Sure, being with Cooper again would be phenomenal, but it could also turn into a monumental disaster and I've had more than my fair share of those lately. Still, as I continued to feel his eyes on me, burning over my skin, I couldn't shake the feeling that it wouldn't be much longer before I metaphorically tapped out. A person could only want something so badly for so long before they finally succumbed to the temptation. And that was Cooper: all temptation.

COOPER

I couldn't keep my eyes off her.

It was just like when we were younger, except my hungry body had gotten a hell of a lot more creative over the last several years with all the ways it could enjoy Haley. It was a fantasy I'd succumbed to from time to time, and now that I'd actually had her in my arms again and tasted her, I wasn't sure how much more I could take.

She was so goddamn beautiful over there with the light of the sunset creating this extraordinary halo over her hair. She'd worn it down tonight and as we'd walked to the town square earlier, I had to fight the urge to reach out and play with the silky strands.

She was truly in her element now, and it made her that much more beautiful. When we were in college, she was still trying to figure out what she wanted to do with her love of art. But later, after we broke up, Tess mentioned Haley had taken a job teaching art to children, and it made perfect sense to me. It was easy to imagine her in a classroom, and as I watched her from across the square, it was clear this was something she loved doing.

Maybe I shouldn't have been watching her so closely, but it wasn't like these booths were all that difficult to construct. I'd been making them with the same group of people for the last couple of years and we had it down to a science. We wouldn't get all of them done tonight, but we were usually finished before the other groups, and it allowed us to assist everyone else.

My eyes kept drifting to Haley, laughing and smiling with the kids. She was a natural with them, and it reminded me of the plans we'd once made for children.

Thankfully, my dangerously wayward thoughts were interrupted by Mahina in my ear. "You know, I don't think you're the only one watching her tonight," she said in a low voice, startling the hell out of me.

Trying to calm my racing heart, I looked at her and breathed out, "Jesus Mahina, you 'bout gave me a heart attack."

She rolled her eyes at me. "Oh please, you're such a drama king." Her not so quiet declaration was met with laughter from the other guys and I glared down at her. She refused to be deterred. "Pay attention to what I'm saying, blockhead. Follow my eyes—six o'clock."

Noting the seriousness of her words, I did as she said and looked straight ahead. Just beyond the square, someone was hiding on the other side of a hedge.

"What the hell?" I muttered as we monitored the stranger. I couldn't tell if it was a man or a woman, but I watched as they raised up an object—a camera—and it was pointing directly at Haley.

I immediately went into action, working my way to the outer edge of the square so I could blend into the crowd and sneak up on whoever it was. Haley may not have been back for long, but she was a part of this community, and Hanalei didn't take kindly to strangers harassing one of her own. *I would not allow her to be harassed... or hurt again.*

I felt that conviction so deeply in my bones that I felt nearly ten feet tall by the time I came upon the man squatting behind the hedge, so focused on his shot that he didn't notice me sneaking up behind him.

The man was snapping pictures rapidly with a camera that had an obscenely long lens zooming in on Haley... *my Haley.*

I snatched the man by his collar, and he cried out. "What the hell do you think you're doing?" I growled.

The man rose to his full stature, which only came up to my chest. "Hey, unhand me, this is assault!"

"No, it's not..." I said, looking into his greasy face, "but it's about to be," I promised, my hands itching to show him how wrong he was to show up here.

I snatched the camera from his neck, the strap ripping loose while the man made a yelping sound like I'd punched him.

That's when Mayor Kahale and Mahina appeared behind the shrub, looking sternly at the intruder.

"Help! I'm being attacked!" the man insisted to the mayor and Mahina, but they were unmoved.

"What? You don't like our welcoming committee?" Mahina asked the man with a grim smile.

"What are you doing here, sir?" the mayor asked the man evenly.

The man was still huffing and puffing dramatically. "I am just doing my job, that's all. I swear there's nothing untoward about what I'm doing."

"That's debatable," Mahina muttered.

"Sir, if your job involves you hiding in the bushes and taking pictures of unsuspecting people, might I suggest you find other, more respectable employment?" Mayor Kahale said.

"Hey don't judge me," the man spat out. "You have the runaway bride over there. Do you know how much money I could get for pictures of her hiding out?" he asked, waving his arms around frantically.

"You mean to tell me your payday is in this little camera?" I asked him, holding up the very expensive piece of equipment.

"Yes!" the man exclaimed.

Maybe I should have given pause, thought about my actions, but I was working off adrenaline. I swung the camera down hard, letting it crash into a million little pieces on the rocky ground.

The mayor and Mahina stepped back to avoid getting hit by debris and the man squawked indignantly. "That was a thousand-dollar camera, I will sue!" he said, pointing an angry finger at me.

I was unmoved and so were Mahina and the mayor. "Well, in order for that lawsuit to have any merit, you will need to have proof and witnesses," the mayor said an even tone, as if he was merely discussing the weather.

"This mess will be cleaned up in no time—and sadly, there are no witnesses. Unless…" he trailed off looking to Mahina, "did you see anything?"

Mahina rubbed her chin dramatically, looking at the crushed camera and shrugged her shoulders. "I have no idea what you're talking about."

"You've got to be kidding me! This corruption!" The man insisted.

"That's the last thing I would worry about if I were you, buddy," I told him tightly. "If you think what I did to that camera is bad, wait until you see what I have planned for you," I warned.

The man's eyes widened and Mahina proclaimed, "I'd listen to him and turn tail, buddy."

The man sputtered as Mahina started counting down. "5… 4…"

"You can't do this!"

"3… 2…"

The man let out a frustrated shriek, then turned and ran.

We watched until he was out of sight, then the mayor calmly pulled his walkie-talkie from his waistband, pressed the button and said, "Officers, be on the lookout for a short, round man running from the square. Kindly make sure he finds his way out of town."

Mahina chuckled, but I was in no laughing mood. "Thank you both for the back-up."

The mayor shook his head. "No need. We take care of our own. Besides, I don't want Haley going home and telling people she wasn't safe here."

Haley going back home.

The thought sat on my chest like a heavy weight. Mahina looked at me oddly. "Cooper? You okay?"

I nodded, swallowing hard around the lump that suddenly formed in my throat. "Yeah, yeah, I'm fine. Just annoyed that guy thought he was going to get away with harassing one of our own."

"Don't worry, I'm sure the HPD will let him know that kind of harassment will not be tolerated around here. Now, let's get back to the planning before anyone notices we're gone."

I was the last one to follow, looking off in the direction the man ran off to, and wondered how much longer Haley would have to put up with this nonsense. It had been several weeks since she'd arrived, long enough for others to find her. I was proud of my fellow residents and how swiftly we handled the intruder. Still, I worried about what Haley was facing—especially once she went home.

There was that thought again, sticking in my chest and making me fidget uncomfortably. "I told you," Mahina said in a sing-song voice, falling into step next to me.

When I looked at her in question, she responded, "you're a goner Cooper, she's in your blood now."

I laughed because what Mahina didn't understand was Haley had been in my blood since we were kids.

Misreading my laugh, Mahina doubled down. "A man doesn't threaten to tear another man apart over a woman he sort of likes," she pointed out.

I shook my head. "It makes no difference, Mahina. Once she's done hiding out, she'll leave us." *Just like she did last time.*

Mahina looked at me like she was dealing with a child. "Well then, think Cooper. What didn't you do last time to get her to stay?" she asked, not waiting for an answer as she left me to contemplate what I could have done differently when Haley and I broke up the first time.

It's not like I hadn't contemplated it a million times before—it was a worry that plagued me often over the last ten years, and it always came back to the same ugly truth: I hadn't fought for her. Sure, I may have protested a little, but mostly I was so dumbstruck by what was happening I'd let her go—way too easily.

I should have fought harder, demanded to know why she was making this mistake. I could have figured out what had her so spooked that she ruined something that was pure magic.

Instead, I listened to my agent and threw myself into my work. I was the first one at the gym and the last one to leave. My teammates and coaches often commented on my intense work ethic, of how football was my life, but there was no room for anything else, by design. Sometimes I wondered what they would think of my rock solid work ethic if they knew it was just my way of pushing what I really wanted out of my head.

These thoughts were rioting in my head as my mini crew and I finished up what we could for the evening, then moved our progress to the back of the community center, covering the booths with tarps for safe keeping.

When I came back to the square, I spied Haley talking to a few of the kids' parents as they helped clean up their progress. I walked up next to her in time to hear her telling the parents that she would set about getting the mural sight prepped during the day and when the kids were available, they would all work on it together. She was gesturing to several drawings the kids made to show their parents what their respective parts would be.

She was in her happy place and for the second time tonight, I was grateful to Mahina for knowing what was best and pushing Haley to be out here.

Once the parents left, she turned to me with bright eyes and a satisfied smile. "That was so much fun—but we have so much work ahead of us," she said, falling into step next to me. She listed off on her fingers everything that needed to be happen before she saw the kids again and I watched her, reveling in the lightness around her.

Her to-do list lasted as long as our walk home and she looked startled when we stopped and she realized we were already on her porch.

She smiled at me. "Thank you, Cooper, for inviting me. I forgot how good it feels to be a part of something."

I tried to smile, but it felt tight as I told her, "Hey, it's mutually beneficial. The festival really needs someone like you."

My words seemed to fall on deaf ears because she was tilting her head, looking at me quizzically. "Cooper? What's bothering you?"

I shook my head. "Nothing."

"Bullshit," she whispered. "Come on, this is me you're talking to. I realize I may not be your favorite person and I understand why, but it's still safe to talk to me."

I sighed. "Haley, it's nothing like that. I'm just worried."

"About what?" she demanded.

"About you," I told her honestly. "I caught some asshat trying to take pictures of you tonight. You were minding your own business, and this guy was hiding in the bushes like a creep snapping pictures of you."

Her shoulders slumped. "Oh," she said, sounding oddly relieved. "That's it?"

"What do you mean, that's it? It's a huge violation of your privacy."

She nodded. "You think I don't know that? I'm not a fan of it either, but to tell you the truth, I'm surprised it took them this long to find me—it was nice while it lasted."

"Would you listen to yourself? You shouldn't have to deal with that. You deserve to be left in peace."

She looked at me patiently, stepping closer so I could see the resignation in her eyes. "I'm not disagreeing with you, Cooper. But I had to accept this as part of the deal when I got engaged to Marcus—there would be photographers and unflattering pictures, and a lack of privacy—no matter how much I hate it."

This whole situation made my blood boil with anger. "That may have been the case before Haley, but you're no longer engaged to that jackass and you're definitely not his wife," I said, spitting out the last two words, hating to refer to her as someone else's wife. "You shouldn't have to deal with this anymore."

She sighed, frustrated. "Cooper, you of all people should know that's not how any of this works. Did they stop hounding you just because you weren't playing anymore?"

"We're not talking about me, Haley..."

"Why not? You had to deal with the press, too. This isn't any different," she insisted.

"The hell it isn't." I argued.

"How?"

"Because I was a famous professional athlete," I growled out, "and now I'm going to have to break the hand of every slimy paparazzi who's trying to make a buck off of you."

She smiled softly at me. "While I appreciate your enthusiasm, it's not necessary. I can take care of myself."

"I know you can, Haley, but I'm asking you to let me help you. You don't have to take on the world alone."

Something flashed in her eyes, and her lips twisted into a wry smile. "That's kind of the point of not sharing your burdens—to protect the ones you love."

"It's a fine line between love and martyrdom."

Her eyes narrowed on me then, and she shook her head. "What would you know about it, Cooper? You can play big and bad protector all you want, but you have no idea what it means to protect someone you love from something that would hurt them. It's not always breaking hands and puffing up with machismo. Most of the time, they're sacrifices no one else sees."

"Don't talk in riddles, Haley. What did you have to sacrifice? I don't believe for a second it was the catastrophe of a wedding you ran away from. We both know damn well you've been running for longer than that."

A tear slipped down her cheek as she shook her head. "Don't go there, Cooper," she warned.

Maybe I should have heeded her warning, but I couldn't seem to stop myself. "No, Haley, you put it out there, so now I want to know what these sacrifices are you speak so cryptically of. What did you give up that hurt you so badly?"

"You!" she spit out, tears falling freely now. "You. Are you happy now? It was you, Coop."

It felt like she'd punched me in the gut. I shook my head in confusion. "What do you mean, me?"

She turned away from me, swiping the tears away from her cheeks. "I thought I was doing the right thing by walking away from you—I thought I'd be in the way."

Her words didn't make any sense. "Why would you ever think that? What did I do to give you that idea?"

She shook her head emphatically. "It doesn't matter anymore," she said.

Anger lit into my confusion. "What do you mean, it doesn't matter? How can you say that?"

"Because Cooper," she said, hiccupping. "That was a lifetime ago. We're not those kids anymore."

"Really? Because I still feel like the kid you left behind, utterly confused by what had gone wrong. And I'm sup-posed to believe it was to protect me? From what?"

She kept shaking her head. "I thought I was doing the right thing, Cooper," she said again. "I can't expect you to understand," she cried out as she started backing away.

I couldn't stand the thought of her backing away from me—not again.

"Haley," I said, reaching for her. Relief swelled inside me when she didn't pull away and I took advantage by pulling her into my arms, resting my forehead against hers. "Make me understand, baby. Tell me what I don't know," I whispered.

"Coop," she croaked, "I'm not even sure if I understand anymore," she whispered, the agony in her voice clear. "Nothing makes sense to me anymore."

My eyes went from her watery gaze to her stress bitten lips. "Nothing?"

She let out a shaky breath. "Well, almost nothing," she amended.

And then we were kissing, wrapped tightly in one another's arms. I reveled in how she clung to me, like she'd never let go—and all I could do was hope she never would.

I drank at her lips, tasting the salt of her tears and ten years of frustration, longing and confusion. It was a relief to know she'd wrestled with the same emotions that had been plaguing me for all this time.

She pulled back from me. "Coop, I can't do it," she started, and my heart fell. "I can't be without you for another second. I need to feel you. I need to be with you, please," she begged, her eyes roving my face with a desperation I recognized all too well—it was what I saw in the mirror every day.

"I'll do whatever you want, Hales, just say the word."

Her breath shuddered as she said, "come to bed with me."

HALEY

N ever would I have dreamed of saying those words to Cooper after pushing him away, but in that moment, my need for him was all-consuming. I was so tired of fighting and when his eyes flashed hot at my request, I knew I'd done the right thing—I would pick up the pieces in the morning.

He answered me by roughly tugging me to him and slanting his mouth across mine, walking me backwards in his embrace until my back rested on the screen door.

I moaned as I leaned into his kiss, so relieved to feel him this close. There was that overwhelming feeling again.

Home.

Tonight I would go home and revel in every second in Cooper's arms.

I stopped him long enough to unlock the door, and he followed me inside, not allowing us to break our touch. His hand stayed clutched at my waist as we moved into the living room and as soon as he closed the door behind him, I was in his arms again, drinking in the taste of him, my hands drifting to the buttons of his shirt. My fingers worked frantically as his mouth attacked my neck, making me gasp as he nipped at the sensitive skin.

Once I undid all the buttons, I shoved the shirt off his shoulders, my heart thundering at the ferocity in his eyes as the shirt fell to the floor and he quickly divested himself of his undershirt.

His chest and abs were even more defined than they were years ago, his muscles honed into finely chiseled grooves. Apparently, surfing was even more effective at keeping him in fine form than football was.

The sound of his husky chuckle brought my attention back to his handsome face. "If I would have known you'd have that reaction, I'd have stripped down a lot sooner," he teased as his hands went to the waistband of his jeans. My hands shot out and stilled them, taking over.

I held his gaze as I undid the snap, then pulled down the zipper of his jeans. He bit his lip in a way that made me want to bite it too and in that moment I decided tonight I wouldn't fight my instincts, so I leaned forward and nipped at his fuller bottom lip. He let out an anguished groan. "I'd forgotten how enthusiastic you can be," he murmured.

I grinned at him. "You haven't seen nothing yet."

His smile matched mine and then his hand cupped the back of my neck, bringing my mouth to his again. "That's my girl," he whispered before kissing me again, his tongue wasting no time tracing the seam of my lips before dipping inside.

I welcomed him in, our feet shuffling us closer to my bedroom as we left a trail of clothes on the floor in our wake. I was so grateful it wasn't far.

When we got to the bedroom, he stopped for a moment, taking in the room he used to sneak into regularly. "My God, this hasn't changed at all," he said.

I stood before him now in my bra and panties and reached behind me to unhook my bra. "The woman it belongs to hasn't changed much either," I reminded him.

His jaw clenched when my bra hit the floor, but when my fingers went to the band of my panties, he jolted out of his frozen position and spurred into action. "Oh no, that's my job," he insisted in a ragged voice, as his fingers slipped beneath the silky fabric and he slid them down my legs. He went down to his knees before me, as I lifted first one foot and then the other to help him get the panties off me.

I didn't realize I was holding my breath until I felt it come out of me in a whoosh when he looked up at me earnestly before he grasping my hips, and bringing me to his mouth. He didn't touch my most sensitive spot, not at first anyway. Instead, he turned his head, resting it against my quivering body, and tightened his arms around my hips and ass. He held me to him, just inhaling me, and I squirmed from the tickle of his five o'clock shadow against my stomach.

When he didn't move for a long moment, I combed my fingers through his hair. "Cooper?" I asked, shifting from foot to foot.

"Mmm? I'm taking my time Haley, you'll just have to cool your jets," he teased.

"Coop," I breathed out in a near whine and felt even more frustrated when I felt and heard his chuckle against me.

"You were always so impatient, my needy girl," he said as he tipped his head back, mirth dancing in his eyes as he gave me a long look before leaning forward and placing the softest of kisses against my stomach right next to my belly button.

"Maybe I just know what I want," I said as I shivered beneath the heat of his lips, needing more. He continued torturing me by leisurely placing kiss after kiss down my body, each one moving lower than the one before until he reached the top of my mound, only to stop and look up at me, then slowly lick back up the same trail of kisses he'd just left behind.

I sighed, throwing my head back in frustration, trying to focus on the sensations his mouth commanded when he abruptly rose, holding me to him and carrying me to the bed. He positioned my ass at the foot of the bed, and then dropped to his knees, a flash of pain showing in his features. "Cooper," I started, worried about his bad knee.

He must have predicted what I was about to say because he shook his head and assured me, "No, Haley, I am right where I want to be."

I looked down at him and compromised, reaching behind me and snatching up a throw pillow. "Fine, at least give yourself some cushion," I said, handing him the pillow. He looked at it slightly offended. "Please?" I added for good measure, not able to stand the idea of him hurting himself over my pleasure.

Reluctantly, he took the pillow and shoved it under his bad knee, eyeing me seductively as I sat before him. That's when his hands went to my knees and spread them apart, baring me to his hungry gaze.

Maybe I should have felt self-conscious, but mostly I felt hot and needy, eager for him to touch me.

His lips stretched into a satisfied smile as he eyed me. "Beautiful," he said as he smoothed his rough palms up the inside of my thighs. "Lean back gorgeous," he directed me and I did as I was told, leaning back on my elbows but keeping a careful eye on him—there was no way I was going to miss one minute of this show.

His fingers petted the sensitive skin at the tops of my thighs but he had yet to touch my center—no he saved that for his mouth which dove forward, kissing and licking my mound then stopping and staring at my pussy as if he was memorizing. I held my breath as he did, only letting it out in a relieved cry when he flicked out his tongue and licked my clit.

His patience must have run out because as his mouth ravaged me, his fingers quickly followed suit, as he slipped first one, and then a second, inside me. "Cooper," I moaned. "Oh my God, that feels so good," I said breathlessly, forcing myself to watch him as he licked and sucked at me, his fingers pistoning in and out of me at a speed that had my head spinning. Between that and his mouth my first orgasm of the night came swiftly, overtaking me before I fully realized it was coming. I cried out in surprise and amid the spasms overtaking me, I could feel his smile against my overly sensitized flesh.

He placed delicate kisses against the insides of my thighs as I came down from my climax, but I wasn't interested in anything delicate at that point. As soon as I caught my breath, I sat up facing him, looking into his satisfied, fiery eyes.

I grabbed his shoulders, urging him back a little so I could stand, reveling in the worshiping look in his eyes as he watched me, like his very breath depended on my next move. I pulled him into a standing position, reaching up and cupping his face, rising on my tip-toes to kiss him, a thrill of excitement racing through me at the feel of his erection against my stomach. My hand drifted down, grasping him in my fingers, and he let out a hiss of anguish against my lips at my first tentative strokes that quickly turned more confident. I watched his face in avid curiosity, loving the emotions playing out there. There was no shyness or hiding with this man. I could give and take pleasure out in the open, soaking up every delicious detail.

"Haley," he growled in warning, and I let out a husky laugh at my power over him. I halted my strokes long enough to reposition him, gently steering him to sit on the bed.

He didn't say a word, just let me put him where I wanted him, sitting up in my bed in all his naked glory, feasting my eyes on the beautiful sight. The corner of his mouth twitched at my ogling, but his expression sobered when I climbed onto the foot of the bed and crawled over his lap on my hands and knees. "I need you inside of me *now*, Coop," I whispered, and I could see how my request affected him as I straddled his lap, his hardness pressed between us.

"You have no idea how many times I've dreamed about you saying that, my sweet Haley." And as I felt him fully against me, his hardness pressed against my wetness, I moaned long and low.

"Goddamn, you keep making sounds like that, Hales, and this will be over before it even starts," he warned in my ear.

I laughed low in my throat. "I have a sneaking suspicion you'll be able to recover and rise to the occasion—you are a world-class athlete, after all."

His eyes found mine in the low light of the room and in all seriousness he said, "Not even that can compare to how badly I want you, you know that, right?"

Not knowing what to say, I kissed him hard, tasting myself on his tongue and delighting in his closeness. I positioned him in between my thighs and the friction made me gasp, but more than ever I needed to be filled by him.

I was hovering over him, looking down into those eyes that haunted both my dreams and waking hours for so long.

Cooper shuttered, "Haley," he whispered before I slid the tip of him inside of me. He let out a curse and smiled, satisfied as I sank myself down inch by glorious inch, stretching me wide and making me moan out.

I waited a moment to adjust to his size, peppering kisses along his jaw, and when I was ready, I moved my hips against his restlessly.

He chuckled against my skin, "Ok needy girl, I'll take the hint," he said, beginning to meet my hips with his and any cohesive thought in my head at that moment floated away taken over by the sensations of this man's desire filling me again and again as his mouth roamed over my neck and cheeks, my back arching when he sucked a hard nipple into his hungry mouth before attacking my other breast.

I had fond memories of our time together when we were younger, but I didn't remember it being this explosive. Maybe it was the intensity in his eyes as I bounced up and down onto him, filling myself with what I craved most. This went way beyond the other times we'd made love—it was possessive and soul-shattering, and I never wanted it to end.

"Haley," he moaned against my mouth, "My sweet girl, you feel so good—so *fucking* good."

I speared my fingers into his hair, bringing his mouth to mine, mimicking what his cock was doing to me. I could feel the spasms building up again, but I wanted him to come with me. "Cooper," I moaned, "Coop, I'm going to come again."

He groaned in response. "Don't worry baby, I'm right there with you," he said, his fingers digging into my frantic hips. "Come for me."

On his command, the spasms I'd been holding off came rushing in full force, my walls squeezing him tightly as my second orgasm hit hard, milking his first one from him. "Fuck," he hissed at his release, clutching my hips as I gently rocked back and forth, enjoying every stroke of our pleasure.

We laid in each other's arms for a long time, as our heart rates returned to normal. No words needed to be spoken. We just needed to be in each other's arms, oblivious to the rest of the world or what was waiting for us.

The next morning I did not awake with Cooper in my bed, but he was still in my house, and—was that hammering?

I rolled over and checked the clock. It was well past the normal time I got up. Sleepily, I slipped from bed and put on my robe, enjoying how my body was sore in places it usually wasn't. After brushing my teeth, I went to investigate the noise and found Cooper on a small ladder outside the front door, fiddling with something over the top of the door.

"Cooper?"

He peeped down at me, "Oh hey, good morning, Sunshine," he said with a broad smile.

"Good morning," I replied, thrilled with the way he eyed my breast at the low neckline of my robe. I was so happy Tess thought to pack this, but then again at the thought of Tess a fresh wave of ancient guilt washed over me.

"What's wrong?" Cooper asked, noticing my expression as he climbed down the ladder and came inside.

I shook my head, pasting on a sunny smile. No need to ruin the moment by bringing up Tess. "It's nothing—other than I woke up in a bed that didn't have you in it."

He grinned at me, pulling me into his arms and giving me a sweet but thorough kiss. When he released me, I said, "Nice attempt at diversion, but you still didn't explain what you were doing to my house."

I could see an ornery twinkle in his eye as he said, "Why don't we make some breakfast to fuel up for the day and I will tell you all about it."

I wasn't sure about his evading the question but breakfast certainly sounded good, so I reluctantly let him lead me to the kitchen where we gathered up some bacon, eggs and some frozen hash browns I had in the freezer.

As Cooper scrambled some eggs, he asked, "You got any Spam?"

I laughed, "You really have acclimated to the island life, haven't you?"

He shrugged. "What? It's delicious with eggs. Are you seriously telling me you don't have a can on hand?" he asked with raised eyebrows.

I answered him by walking over to the small pantry and producing a can.

"Atta girl," he smiled as he grabbed it from me, "We might just make an island girl out of you yet."

I smiled even though it caused a brief tightness in my chest that I wasn't interested in examining too closely.

We made breakfast in companionable silence, enjoying bumping into one another in the small kitchen and finding excuses to touch one another. Cooper was the only man I couldn't seem to keep my hands off of and now that we'd reunited, my hands had a renewed thirst for him.

I refrained from asking about the hammering and the ladder until we sat with our breakfast at the small kitchen table. "Alright Mr. Handyman—which is a totally hot look on you, by the way—what gives with the banging around this morning?"

He hastily wiped at his mouth before leveling his gaze at me. "Just hear me out…"

"Oh no," I said, already not liking the sound of whatever this was going to be.

"It's one of those doorbell cameras that's attached to an app on your phone," he explained.

I scoffed. "Come on, Cooper. I don't want one of those things. For God's sake, I don't think there's a soul in town who has one of those things."

He worked to swallow the food he'd been chewing, contemplating what to say next. "That may be true, Hales. But there's also nobody else in town who has random strangers taking pictures of them so they can make a buck."

Not this again. "Cooper, I thought we hashed this out last night."

"We did… briefly, before we started making out," he reminded me.

I couldn't help the blush that overtook my cheeks. "Oh... that's right, we got a little distracted from the topic at hand."

"More than a little..." he winked, and I laughed.

"Come on Cooper, I never took you for a man who needed that much ego-stroking," I said, reaching across the table to stroke his jaw. "Besides," I said, dropping my voice, "I would've thought the multiple answers you provided were more than enough evidence of that."

I leaned across the table to give him a quick peck and his eyes fell to my robe, that was falling open. "I think I'm getting distracted again," he said as I laughed against his lips, happy to welcome the distraction. Nothing like a little morning nookie with the most gorgeous man alive whose hand was slipping beneath my short, silky robe...

He moaned into my mouth. "Haley, did you not bother to put panties on?"

I laughed, "Now what would the point be in that?"

I delighted in the heat that stole over his features as he smiled with pride at me and teased, "I like the way you think, my naughty girl."

He kissed me then, sweet and slow, and it felt like time stood still. Our hands roamed all over each other, exploring the places we might have missed the night before, not caring that our breakfast was growing cold. Cooper hefted me up into his arms and was about to carry me back to bed when the landline rang.

I squirmed until he put me down. "The only one who calls that line is Tess," I said apologetically as I reached for the phone. It's probably nothing major, just her daily check-in, but I wasn't going to ignore my dearest friend who'd been worried sick about me and stuck out her neck to help me over the last few weeks.

There was that guilt again. I choked it back as I answered the phone. "Hello?"

"Haley," Tess answered, not bothering with a hello and sounding slightly out of breath.

"Tess? Are you okay?" I asked, as she didn't sound like herself. Cooper watched me intently, concern washing over his expression.

"Yeah, yeah. I'm fine. I'm sorry I sounded so weird, it's just that—well, I had a bizarre conversation and I'm still processing it all, but I snuck away to call you the second I could."

"Sounds serious. What's going on?"

I could hear her sucking in a deep breath, "Well, the media attention on the 'runaway bride' has hit a fever pitch. I didn't want to tell you how bad it had gotten because I knew you needed to focus on yourself—and honestly, I figured it would've died down after a few days, but then..." she trailed off.

"But then what?" My heart rate picked up a in panic.

She sighed, "But then Marcus started giving these tearful interviews about how he's the jilted groom and he should have seen it coming. He actually implied you were only with him for his money since you're on a school teacher salary."

My whole body was tense. "That asshole," I breathed, and that's when I realized Cooper was by my side now, waiting for the signal that he needed to do something.

"I know," Tess lamented, and I could tell in her voice how frustrating this had to be for her. I'd been in Hanalei having sexy fun with her older brother while she was putting out fires on my behalf back home. I felt like the worst friend ever. "It gets worse. You know all those reporters who have been hounding you for interviews? Well, somehow one of them got my cell number—I just got off the phone with them."

I growled out in frustration. "My God, they won't quit. Tess, I am so sorry you're having to deal with this. That's crossing the line."

"Haley, listen to me. I'm not worried about that. The reason I called you is that this reporter offered a very intriguing sum of money and, by intriguing I mean ridiculously large. I know you've had a couple of crazy offers, but with the way Marcus is trying to spin this and smear your reputation, I think it's time for you to..."

"Tess, no..." I started. There's no way she's going to suggest what I think she is.

"Hales, look, normally I wouldn't suggest it, but hell, you should get something for your trouble. Consider it reparations for your pain and suffering. And it is only fair you should get to say your piece—why should he get to have his cake and eat it too?"

"Tess..."

"Just think about it, okay? I know it's out of your comfort zone. But I think you should defend yourself against this jackass. Think about it, please?"

I sighed. "Fine, I will think about it, but I can't promise anything."

"Understood," she said.

"And Tess?"

"Yeah?"

"I really appreciate everything you've done—looking out for me and everything," I said, struggling to get the words out around the lump in my throat.

"Haley, quit thanking me for that—it's what best friends are for."

I bit my lip, desperately trying to hold my emotion in check. "I know," I said, barely above a whisper. We said our goodbyes, and I hung up the phone.

Cooper didn't ask questions. He didn't need to. My face clearly showed the exhaustion and betrayal I felt from dealing with the Marcus situation.

Still, I assured him Tess was fine.

"I gathered that," he said simply.

"A reporter tracked down her number trying to get my side of the story," I added.

His jaw tensed before he answered, "I gathered something along those lines too."

It was coming back to me now, how Cooper could be a man of few words in stressful situations and how much that used to drive me crazy when we were younger. Apparently, it still drives me crazy.

After a long, tense moment, he said, "It sounds like they're getting more aggressive—now that they're going after my sister."

I nodded. "I hate that they're dragging her into this."

"I know, and I'm not blaming you for that. But this reiterates my point, Haley. First the guy who was taking pictures and now this, you need to be more cautious. Is Marcus stirring shit up?"

I didn't want to answer that, but he deserved the truth, especially since it involved Tess now. "According to Tess, he's given multiple interviews crying wolf. I'm not surprised—it's always election season as far as he's concerned."

"To hell with his election season. He doesn't have the right to destroy you just because he's pissed," he fumed.

I shook my head. "I don't care about what Marcus does."

He cut in. "Really? Because it seems like an excellent time to care. This guy needs to be put in his place. He's playing with fire here."

I sighed. "Look, I get that you're being protective, and it's sweet, but I don't think it's necessary to get this upset. He's a pain in the ass, but ultimately harmless."

Cooper shook his head at me. "Yeah, just like that creep who flew all the way to the island to take pictures of you is harmless."

"Cooper, it's not like he actually hurt me."

"Only because I threatened certain dismemberment if he came near you again. I mean, shit, what is it going to take to make you take this more seriously?"

I barked out a laugh. "This is my life, and I assure you I take it very seriously, but I am sick of people telling me how I need to live it. I'm not going to live in fear over what others are saying about me when I know it's lies—they don't matter."

He let out a long sigh, looking defeated but knowing Cooper I'm right to be suspicious when he gave in that quickly. That wasn't the man I remembered. "Well, if you're going to be thinking about whatever it Tess wants you to think about, then let me pile on and add you need to reconsider security around here."

"Good God, you Barclays are relentless," I mumbled.

"Yes we are," he grinned, leaning over and kissing me on the head. "But you love us anyway," he added, stiffening slightly when he realized what he said.

There was an awkward silence, then Cooper straightened and turned away. "I'll just, uh, clean up these dishes..." he trailed off as he grabbed our dishes and headed into the kitchen.

"Yeah," I said, letting him off the hook. I knew his slipping in the 'L' word was purely accidental, but his reaction was not and a curious mixture of warmth and worry tightened in my chest.

We cleaned up in silence as I tried not to overthink everything that had taken place in the last twenty-four hours. I needed some time to think—alone.

"Listen, I'm going to get dressed and head to the General Store since Mahina promised she would hook us up with supplies for the festival. I want to have everything ready to go for the kids."

Cooper nodded, seeming to understand I needed some time, and not just to gather art supplies. "Right, that's okay, I have a session with a client in an hour so... I'll see you later?" he asked hopefully.

I smiled at him, leaning in close to give him a long, slow kiss. "Yeah... it's a date."

COOPER

The waves sure as hell had their work cut out for them today. While they usually calmed and centered me, after everything that went down with Haley and the way my head was swirling, I needed to take some of my angst out on the water.

I did my best to compartmentalize when I was with my client and focus on what they needed, but my mind kept reliving last night, filled with long caresses, deep kisses and pleasure so hot it could melt the sun.

Haley still wasn't back at her bungalow by the time I was done, and I tried not to let it bother me. She was perfectly capable of taking care of herself, and Hanalei was relatively safe. Plus, everyone knew her now and would keep an eye out. It's what people did around here—especially Mahina, which was who Haley was with.

I'd always been protective. It came with the territory of being an older brother, but now I felt downright overbearing, and I couldn't seem to help it. Every time I remembered catching that sleazebag taking pictures of Haley, I got a sick feeling in my gut. Haley may not have thought much of it, but it was haunting me, along with whatever was going on in San Diego that had Tess calling with concern.

Putting my board up, I went into my house and looked around, contemplating my next move. Then I gave in and did what I'd promised myself I would never do since Haley came back to Hanalei: I did an internet search of her ex.

I reasoned I needed to know how much trouble might be brewing here. If it was enough to have Tess worried, then I had to cause to worry, too.

What met my eyes had my stomach instantly turning. The ex-fiancé looked like most politicians: classically handsome but smarmy and full of shit. He appeared to be doing his best impersonation of a Kennedy, but he clearly lacked charisma.

The first few headlines featured video clips and sound bytes of a teary Marcus telling the interviewer he didn't know what went wrong and he'd been totally blindsided. And then there were pictures. One of Marcus and Haley together looking forcefully happy for the cameras, though I could see how posing for the camera was a strain for her. She hated that sort of attention. But in each picture, she dutifully stood next to Marcus and represented him well. I was down the rabbit hole now, and more pictures appeared. Slightly blurry ones that were taken from a distance of Marcus and a mystery blonde he was making out with. The pictures were dated two weeks before the wedding was to have taken place.

"Piece of shit," I muttered, shaking my head. Tess had been careful to spare me the details of what made Haley run, but now it was coming together. She must have discovered he was a cheating bastard right before the ceremony.

I kept scrolling. There was a video entitled "Runaway Bride." I couldn't help but click the link. According to the caption beneath the video, the press had captured video footage of Haley in all her bridal glory, along with my little sister in her dreadful maid of honor dress, running out of the church like their asses were on fire and hailing a car.

I couldn't help but laugh at the sight because Haley was clearly using her old track skills the way she high-tailed it out of there. Whoever put up the video added music in the background and The Chicks' song "Ready to Run" played as the harried bride and her dutiful maid of honor disappeared inside a sleek, black car that raced off.

So many emotions were warring inside of me. Worry, rage at her ex, and pride in Haley and my sister. Leaving like that could not have been easy. It was no wonder she kept running all the way to Hanalei. I couldn't blame her for getting as far away from that son of a bitch as possible.

And she'd ended up straight in my arms.

But I couldn't focus on that right now, or I'd end up at her door like some panting puppy and I needed to process everything I'd just read.

I spent too much time looking at the myriad of head-lines and quotes from Marcus implying that Haley was only marrying him for money. I would have continued torturing myself if it wasn't for my phone ringing. It was my agent.

"Hey Bo, this isn't a good time."

"What are you talking about, kid? This is a great deal I got cooked up for you. We need to talk about what you're going to say to the interviewers."

"That's if I decide I even want to do it," I cut in.

Bo scoffed. "Why on earth wouldn't you do it? This is a gem of a deal. I mean, you would have killed for this two years ago."

I sighed. "I know that Bo, and I appreciate how hard you worked for that, but I'm not sure... a lot has changed in the last two years."

"This is just stage fright," Bo insisted. "You've been out of the public eye for a couple years and you're nervous about being front and center again, that's all."

I was silent for a moment before I said, "Yeah.. . maybe."

"Look, I know it feels scary to you after everything you've been through but you've got to get back in the saddle—and hell, at least they're offering you a saddle, they could have left you out to pasture."

I snickered, because that's exactly how it's felt for the last two years. I was the golden boy of football for most of my career and the second my body failed me, I was dumped and forgotten.

"So I'll arrange the plane tickets and we'll fly you in for an interview by the end of the week," Bo said.

I was quiet as he went on detailing his strategy of what to say during the interviews when I moved the mouse on my computer to close the browser with Haley's heartbreak all over it, but in doing so the mouse rolled over the video clip preview showing Haley running, her veil flying behind her, her big fluffy skirt hooked over her arm as she ran away from everything that was wrong for her back to Hanalei... and me.

At least that's what I liked to think.

Bo rambled on, and I had to interrupt to get a word in edge wise. "Bo? Slow down, man. Listen, I know you want to get this buttoned down, but... I need more time to think about it."

Bo exhaled loudly over the phone. "What is going on with you, kid? Your focus isn't there anymore—what's going on?"

"Nothing, I have a friend who's going through a rough time that I need to help with, and then I can make a more clear-headed decision about this."

"Jesus, don't tell me this 'friend' is a woman. Remember what I always told you, Cooper, women come and go, but opportunities like this are rare—and they don't break your heart. It's like when that one broad left you—she was taking the edge off your game. You can't afford to be distracted. You've got too much going for you, my boy."

I knew Bo was just doing his job and what he thought was best for me, but I wasn't some young kid who could be that easily persuaded. "I don't know what to tell you, Bo... I need more time, so they'll have to wait or pass. I'm not going to make a half-baked decision—there's too much at stake right now."

And as I spoke the words, I knew they would never be more true. I had no idea what Haley was thinking about us and our future, but I knew that this time around, I was going to fight for what I wanted. And I wanted Haley.

HALEY

A month ago, I never would have envisioned myself running at top speed in a big, fluffy wedding dress straight to Hanalei—and Cooper's arms.

But now we were in this weird honeymoon-like situation and I had to work extremely hard to not overthink things and just enjoy myself.

In Hawaiian it's called Manawa: living in the moment. It's not something that comes easily to me, despite growing up spending summers on the island. But if I embraced it, I could enjoy these sweet moments with Cooper, and not fret over how this would all inevitably fall apart or how to explain this to Tess.

I've had moments where flames of panic washed over me as my mind tried to figure everything out, but then I remembered where I was and how lucky I was to be here. Not to mention how strange all of this was. I mean, what were the odds that after my engagement crashed and burned so spectacularly and I came back to my favorite place in the world, I would land straight in the arms of the man I'd never stopped loving?

When I'd walked away from Cooper all of those years ago, I knew I would always love him, regardless of where our lives took us. That truth hasn't changed with time, which is why I'm all too aware that I'm playing with fire here.

But all I wanted to do was enjoy every stolen kiss, every late-night walk on the beach, every spark of pleasure wrought from Cooper's hands because God, his hands had only gotten better with age.

Plus, I couldn't deny that I was enjoying sex more. It's not that sex with Cooper hadn't been absolutely fantastic when we were younger, but we both had more experience and knew what we liked better now. I also had the courage to tell him what I wanted and needed, and he was more than happy to oblige.

In fact, I was so busy reminiscing about the last time we'd been intimate, I didn't realize I'd practically floated into the General Store.

"You're back for more?!" Mahina called as I came through the front door.

I laughed. "Perhaps... or maybe I just need groceries for myself," I answered. Mahina had been more than gracious to offer her stock at the store for materials for the mural and I'd definitely taken advantage of it. She was pretty surprised when I promised her I did indeed need the three pounds of kidney beans for this project.

She came into view, giving that stern smile of hers. "I would complain that you're just taking advantage of my generosity, but I have to admit, I took a peek at the mural this morning when I went to drop some things off at the community center."

My eyes widened. "And?" I asked anxiously. I was extremely proud of what the kids had come up with so far, so nerves raced through me as I waited for Mahina's critique.

Her smile grew broader. "It's even more than I could have wished for. I mean, I have to admit, I was worried when you told me the beans were for the project, but to see what you're doing with them, it's amazing. I was expecting hand prints and doodles, but this is really elevated."

I couldn't help the warm feeling that spread over me. "It was their idea. I just helped them sketch it out, but they're the ones making this happen and I couldn't be prouder. They're a great group of kids." Every time I think about the day when we can finally unveil the piece to the town of Hanalei at the Aloha Festival, I get so giddy I feel like dancing.

"You have a natural talent for getting the best out of them. I can see why you're an art teacher. But I have a confession, Haley: I wasn't the only one taking a peek at your work."

"Oh?"

"Mayor Khaled got a look too, and he wants to talk to you about it."

Worry threaded through me. "You don't think he approves of it?" I asked, prepared to defend that piece to the death because I knew how hard the kids had been working on it.

Mahina smiled, "I doubt it's anything like that, Haley. All he said was the next time I saw you to send you his way when you had a moment."

"Oh," I said, still uncertain. I hadn't really gotten to know Mayor Khaled since I'd been back, so I didn't know what to expect, but if Mahina was unfazed by his request, then I would take my cues from her.

"How's your hunk next door doing?" Mahina asked as she rang up my groceries.

I felt myself blush.

"I'll take that as a good," she said.

"You'll have to ask him yourself."

She tsked. "Please, every time I see that boy, he looks like he's floating on air, grinning from ear to ear, telling me he doesn't kiss and tell."

"Well, that's a good policy to follow."

Mahina rolled her eyes. "Y'all are no fun. Don't you know half the fun of doing anything around here is blabbing about it later?"

I bit my lip. Part of me wanted to sing out from the rooftops I was happy again, that I was having the best sex of my life with a man who didn't need a roadmap to my clitoris, but what was happening between Cooper and me was our little secret and for now, I was going to enjoy guarding it.

Mahina shoved my bag of groceries toward me looking expectant, and then playfully irritated when I merely thanked her and smiled coyly before grabbing my groceries and leaving.

The Town Hall was just across the road and a few doors down, so I crossed the quiet street, groceries in hand and made my way to the mayor's office, thinking all the while how delighted Mahina would be if she knew the details of what was going on between me and Cooper.

"Good morning, ma'am," a young woman called from the front desk.

"Hi, I was told to drop by to speak with the mayor. My name is Haley Ellis."

"Oh! You're the one helping the kids with the mural. My niece Leela is in that group. She can't stop talking about how much fun she's having."

"That's awesome," I smiled. "Leela is such a natural talent."

The receptionist beamed. "She is, but it's been so hard to get her to come out of her shell. I'm glad she feels comfortable enough with you to let her talent shine."

Before I could respond, Mayor Khaled appeared. "Ms. Ellis, I'm so happy you could stop by."

He reached out, shaking my hand, "Mayor, please call me Haley."

"Haley, it is then. I wanted to thank you for your dedicated work with the kids. I've been getting a lot of good feedback from their parents and I'm quite impressed by what I saw at the community center."

"Well thank you, but that's the kids' hard work," I said swiftly, but he was quick to dismiss that idea.

"Haley, let me level with you. I've known most of those children for their whole lives and while they are talented, they haven't excelled until you came on along. So it's got me thinking…"

I raised a questioning eyebrow, not sure where he was going with this. "Our public school is quite small, and the budget is not big enough for an art teacher. But there is a budget for an instructor at the community center. Ironic, I know, considering the repairs it requires, but I'm sure I don't have to explain how archaic and nonsensical town allocations can be. That's something I'm trying to change, but that's not the point I'm trying to make."

"At the risk of sounding rude, Mayor, what is the point?" I asked, eager to know what he was getting at. Mayor Khaled seemed like a genuinely nice man, but I was a little burnt out on circular political talk because of Marcus. I very much wanted him to cut to the chase.

"I'm asking you to consider teaching some art classes at the community center whenever you're available."

I stood there silent for a moment because I didn't know what to say. I was flattered, of course, but—would that mean staying in Hanalei permanently?

"Well, I, uh… I'm very flattered Mayor Khaled, but I still haven't decided what my long-term plans are."

He looked at me thoughtfully. "Well, I was certainly hoping we could make a citizen out of you yet, but I'd be willing to settle for classes for a few weeks. At least it would be something for the kids and adults alike to take part in. I can't tell you how many of those kids' parents have expressed an interest in learning how to do what you're teaching their children."

I felt all the warm tingles over the compliment, but still, "Oh, I don't think it's anything they couldn't learn from a YouTube video."

That's when the mayor leveled his case at me. "With all due respect, Haley, you're wrong. I've seen that mural you're working on with the kids, and it encapsulates the spirit of Hanalei. The kids are really taking pride in what it means to be a part of this town and to be a part of the island. I don't think they could've gotten that from any video online. It took someone who had just as much appreciation for this place to help them express the love for their home."

I felt tears prick the back of my eyes. It wasn't like I didn't get the occasional compliment at the school I worked at and I loved working with the kids, but I had to admit being here with these kids felt different. They were so eager to learn, and I'm guessing part of that was the novelty of it. There wasn't an art program in their school, but they had such beautiful inspiration in their homeland.

I nodded then. "Well, in that case, I think we could make a couple of days a week work. Would that be sufficient?"

The mayor grinned. "That would be perfect."

Little by little, I was becoming part of the fabric of Hanalei, and surprisingly, I loved it. I always thought I enjoyed being anonymous in San Diego. For the most part, people left me alone, didn't expect too much from me, and they definitely didn't ask me any probing questions. It was comforting to know all of my neighbors' names and most of their life stories and that they knew mine.

I'm sure they talked about me behind my back, as is common in small towns, but I never got the sense it was mean spirited. They were just talking and Lord knows it was a juicy story so if it were me, I'd gossip about it too. So I let them go on about it as long as I didn't have to relive it for the millionth time.

As I left the mayor's office, my phone buzzed, and I glanced at it, seeing it was a California number. It looked like the same one from the journalist who has been trying to convince me to do a sit-down interview about Marcus. Despite his relentless attempts, I couldn't bring myself to block his number and I didn't know why.

I hit the decline button and made my way home. When I ran into Cooper, who was waxing his board after a lesson with a client, I stopped short. "Hi, beautiful," he said with a smile, and my stomach flipped. He said it so casually, and yet I believed every word. There was no spin, no manipulation. Cooper meant what he said, and said what he meant, and I missed having somebody in my life who I could trust to be that transparent.

My smile must've faltered because Cooper looked concerned. "What? You don't like me calling you beautiful now?"

I shook my head. "No, I just remembered something... a chore I need to take care of."

"Can it wait? I have plans for you," he said, striding over to me with a mischievous look in his eyes.

I raised a questioning brow. "Oh, yeah? What did you have in mind? Oh, is it for dinner? Because I already have something planned for us."

He slipped his arms around my waist. "Actually, I was thinking more for dessert... come to think of it, maybe we should just have dessert first," he said, leaning down and kissing me sweetly on the lips. His kiss quickly turned from sweet to deep and passionate.

I never imagined I would be having a full-on make-out session on the front porch of my bungalow with Cooper like I was a teenager again, but I also didn't care. I'm sure the neighbors have seen all sorts of kisses and hugs and pats on the butt over the last few days, which might explain the winks and the shy smiles I'd gotten from the occasional neighbor in town.

They seemed genuinely happy for us. This wasn't something I was used to. In Marcus's world, everyone was super competitive. If they saw someone who was really happy, they'd want to know how and why it hap-pened, and why they weren't feeling the same way.

We quickly moved into my living room, and I took over, yanking him by the hand to the couch and then gently pushing him down. "I *really* like this take-charge side of you," he said in a low, rumbly voice.

"Good, because I don't think she's going anywhere," I said, as I slid off my panties and hiked my skirt up so I could straddle his lap.

His eyes searched mine before he said, "Promise?"

I felt my heart pick up faster. I wanted to make that promise but I couldn't, so I answered by kissing him, nipping at his full bottom lip and rejoicing in the groan that tore from his throat.

I couldn't promise Cooper anything long-term right now, but I could promise him all of my love and attention for the time being.

Our hands were everywhere, and I don't remember when or how we got his trunks off but the next thing I knew his engorged purple tip was poised at my opening, and Cooper looked at me, red faced and biting his lip, eager for me to make my next move.

I was enjoying teasing him as I swiveled my hips over him and his fingertips bit into the flesh of my hips. "Hales," he growled out in warning.

I gave him a wicked grin before I slowly sank down over him, inch by inch. "Fuck Hales," he bit out, letting out a long, low moan. I joined in with my own when I was finally seated completely, sitting still for a moment and enjoying how full he made me feel.

"Goddamn you feel so good," he breathed.

I kept his face in my hands, rubbing the pad of my thumb over his lip, then leaning my forehead against his and looking deeply into his eyes. I smiled and said, "Just you wait."

He laughed, but quickly stopped when I started moving my hips, slowly, methodically, gradually picking up speed until my fingers were biting into the skin of his shoulders, holding on for dear life and relishing the way his jaw clenched as he tried to hold on to his release as I rode him feverishly.

"I want to feel you come inside of me," I whispered.

He nodded in confirmation as I watched him grit his teeth, and I knew he was close.

My own release was barreling down on me, my pussy spasming around him. He gripped my hips and pounded into me, exploding just as I couldn't take it anymore, and came, crying out his name, "Cooper!"

I buried my face in his neck, shivering beneath his heated words, "That's it, Hales. That's my good girl... so fucking good, every time."

We stayed on the couch in each other's arms for a while before hunger drove us to clean up and set about making our dinner. We would enjoy more dessert later.

And this became the routine of our days. If Haley from a few months ago had known that good food, great sex, and unexpected friendship were in her future, she would've laughed at the suggestion.

But I was here, and I was going to make the most of it.

I started my classes at the community center a couple of days later, and even though I was nervous at first, it all felt so natural. I taught children and adults alike, and it was so refreshing to have people who were eager to learn something new—and to discover they had talent too. The wonder in their eyes when they made their first works of art was addictive. That would never get old for me.

I spent a week in my blissed out little bubble with Cooper, enjoying his attention and affection, enjoying my newfound community, and feeling like I was back to my old self for the first time in a very long time.

Considering my recent past, I should've known something would pop that bubble sooner than later. When I came up on my porch one afternoon after going to the General Store and checking in with Mahina, I nearly shrieked out in surprise when I found Marcus waiting for me on the front porch.

He looked woefully out of place in his three-piece suit and tie—he had to be hot as hell in his uniform. The weather recently turned muggy, so that tie had to feel like it was choking him.

Thankfully, I saw him before he saw me, so I had a moment to compose myself, peering out to the water to see that Cooper was engrossed in a lesson with a client.

I didn't know what I hoped for more: that he wouldn't notice Marcus was here and lose his shit, or he would help me run this asshole out of town because Marcus was the last person I wanted to deal with.

Finally, I forced my feet to move, addressing Marcus when I hit the bottom of my porch stairs. "Marcus?"

He stood in a rush, a well-practiced smile plastering his mouth. "Haley, it's so good to see you."

I did not return his sentiment as I ascended the stairs. "What are you doing here?"

He appeared a little miffed that I didn't seem equally excited to see him. "Well, I'm here for you, of course. I know things have been... messy for lack of a better word.

But I thought it was time we sat down like adults and hashed this out."

I looked at him, confused. "I don't know what there is to hash out. We were going to get married. I saw you fucking your assistant. So I decided not to marry you and left... end of story. What else could we possibly discuss?"

I saw a flicker of irritation flash in Marcus's eyes and then saw him pull the move I'd witnessed so many times before when he was dealing with a difficult political foe. He'd take a moment, smooth his fingers over his tie while he took a deep breath and then rearranged his features to be more conciliatory and amiable. I was getting the full congressman treatment here, and I didn't like it one bit.

"Haley, please, there's a lot of history between us. You make it sound simple. Like it's over, just like that, but... I still love you."

I laughed. "Marcus, I can honestly say I don't think you've ever loved me."

"Haley, don't be silly."

"No, Marcus, it's true. It's not all your fault because I was never completely myself around you. To tell you the truth, I haven't been myself in a very long time. But I've spent the last few weeks working to change that, to feel more like myself again. To be someone I could be proud of."

His brow furrowed in confusion, and I could tell this was not what he had been expecting. "What are you talking about? You are someone I could be proud of. You looked beautiful on my arm and you always presented yourself so graciously."

"I'm not talking about that. None of that matters to me. I'm talking about someone who I can be proud of," I insisted. "If the man I'm with can be proud of me and brag about me, then fine, but that doesn't amount to much if I can't look myself in the mirror and it's been a long time since I've been able to do that. But not anymore. I'm liking what I see and she's not the woman you knew."

He was silent for a long moment before he blew out of breath and said in a frustrated voice, "Well shit, Hales, where do I fit into all this?"

I straightened my stance and looked him in the eye when I said, "You don't, Marcus. It's over and I think it's what's best for both of us. Deep down, you know that."

His mask was slipping and I could see panic and irritation warring in his eyes before he bit out, "Well, what am I supposed to do now? I have all these people up my ass who want to know where the runaway bride is. How the hell am I'm going to fix this? You have no idea what kind of pickle you've put me in."

I rolled my eyes. "I have no doubt you'll be able to find a way out of it. Besides, did you honestly think I was blind to the interviews you've been giving, the ones that suggest I was unhinged and unstable? Surely that would be the only explanation for somebody running out on you..."

His face reddened. "So what? Now you're saying I wasn't good enough for you? How dare you?"

I had to bite back a laugh at his indignation. He definitely has that dramatic flair working for him. "What? Know what's best for me? Come on Marcus, you know we're not right for each other. When I walked in on you and Skylar, as much as it shocked and pissed me off, I thought to myself that she just makes more sense."

"What the hell are you talking about?" He asked.

"I mean, you and I were never a good match. I don't know why you decided I would be acceptable to you, but I've come to realize why I picked you, and I'm not proud of the reasons."

"So my manager was right? You were using me for influence and power?"

I rolled my eyes. "Oh, come on, you know me well enough to know I don't have any patience for that nonsense. If I did, do you think I'd be hiding out somewhere that's so hard to find me? If that were my goal, I'd be shouting off the rooftops."

His shoulder slumped, and I knew he couldn't disagree. "If I'm being honest, I think I was afraid to be alone. And I enjoyed your company. You can be quite charming when you want to be. But looking back, I wasn't in any position to jump into a relationship so soon after my parents died. I'm not proud of the way I ran out on our wedding... but then again, I didn't enjoy finding you with Skylar, so I guess we can call it even."

Marcus's expression softened briefly before it hardened again. "Well, it's not that simple, Haley. It's an election year. This story hardly helps my poll numbers. You know as well as I do, married candidates fare better."

He was really showing his colors now. "I'm sure you'll find a way to spin it, Marcus."

He shook his head. "I was hoping I would not have to do this, Haley, but since you refuse to cooperate, I'm going to have to tell my PR people to unleash the full treatment."

Something about the last two words sounded ominous. "Full treatment? What does that mean?"

He sighed as if it pained him to say it, although we both knew better. "It means my credibility needs to be built back up and..."

"And that can't be done without tearing mine down, right?"

I shook my head in disbelief. "You know, we both made mistakes in this relationship and if you had an ounce of maturity, we could both just move on, but you have to fight dirty because of your bruised ego."

He let out a long-suffering sigh, looking at me condescendingly. "Really, Haley? You knew what you were getting into when you started dating me and you must have known that pulling that stunt on our wedding day would not go unpunished. While you believe you've been hiding away, all you've been doing is whetting the appetite of the ravenous media to put a noose around the neck of the newest congressman. You know better than to actually believe we can just—how did you put it? Move on? That's not how I roll."

I was about to light into him about "how he rolled" when I heard a deep, angry voice behind us, rushing up the stairs, "You're about to see how someone bigger and scarier rolls motherfucker," and there was Cooper in an explosion of fists as Marcus crumbled down into the seat by my front door.

"Cooper!" I cried out, but Cooper wasn't done.

He fisted Marcus's tie and brought him up so they were nose to nose. "If you ever come near her or speak to her that way again, you're going to get much worse than a broken nose. Do you understand me?"

"Cooper," I tried to break through to him, but he was incapable of hearing me. He was singularly focused on the arrogant man with a bloody nose, staring up at him in fear. "Stop, please, this isn't necessary."

He let go of Marcus long enough to turn to me in angered surprise. "What do you mean, this isn't necessary? I heard him threatening you, Haley."

Marcus was already on the move, putting much-needed space between him and Cooper. "I wasn't threatening her, you dumb oaf. I was merely laying out the consequences of her actions. It's the least I could do after everything she's pulled. And you can expect to hear from my lawyers for medical expenses," he spewed out with vitriol as he held his nose, backing down the steps.

"Then you can expect to hear from my lawyer about harassment and trespassing," Cooper said.

That's when Marcus stopped and looked between the two of us. "So this is why you don't want to come back. You found yourself a little surfer fuck boy, huh? Well, I hope you're happy Haley, and I hope you'll be particularly happy when I sue you both. You," he said, pointing a finger at Cooper, "for assault, and you," he said, pointing a finger at me, "for alienation of affection. I'll see you in court."

I would've laughed if I wasn't so upset with Cooper.

As soon as Marcus was out of sight, I wheeled on Cooper. "What the hell was that?"

Cooper looked shocked. "What do you mean? He was threatening you—and he was close enough to put his hands on you."

"He wouldn't have done that. He's an idiot, but he's smart enough not to get assault charges on him."

"Are you seriously upset with me for defending you?" Cooper asked in disbelief.

He looked so earnest and hurt and angry that I couldn't take it anymore. I turned around and stomped into the house with him hot on my heels. "Haley, answer me," he insisted.

"Yes, I'm upset with you. I don't need to be defended. I'm a big girl. I can handle these things myself."

He let out a frustrated growl. "I never said you couldn't," he insisted, and I thought for a moment he was going to stomp his foot. "But dammit, Haley, you can let people help you every once in a while. You don't have to do everything all by yourself."

"I know that Cooper, but Marcus is my problem, not yours," I said, squaring up to him, needing him to understand I didn't need him coming in like a white knight trying to fix all my problems.

But Cooper's stubborn ass wasn't getting it. "I cannot believe you're actually more upset with me than that douchebag."

"That's because I expect more from you than I do from him, because he is, after all, a douchebag."

"I don't understand what you want from me. I only did what any man would do for someone he loves. Did you want me to just run away?" he spit out, looking at me with wide eyes. We both stopped and straightened. Cooper's mouth snapped shut, his jaw clenching.

His words warred inside me as I looked him dead in the eye and said, "You have no idea what I've had to sacrifice for the people I love and it's clear to me now that you never will... get out."

His jaw unclenched, his face registering surprise. "Are you kidding me?"

"No, I think it's pretty obvious I'm not in a kidding mood. Get. Out."

He shook his head, then turned on his heel and stormed out of the house, the screen door slamming behind him with a finality that made my heart ache.

I found my way to the couch on shaky legs and then plopped down, waiting for the tears to come, but they never came.

As I sat there, I couldn't help but notice the room was almost exactly mirroring what I was feeling, because with each passing second, the room grew darker and darker.

It took me entirely too long to realize that the sky had turned a dangerous shade of green in the time it took to have it out with Marcus and then Cooper. The sunny, peaceful morning I enjoyed earlier was now a gloomy afternoon, and the wind had picked up.

I peeked out the back window and some of the neighbor's kids' toys left in the yard were now flying through the air. "What the..."

There was a storm coming, and it wasn't just the one in my heart.

COOPER

All I wanted to do was storm back into Haley's house, snatch her up into my arms and drag her to the bedroom and show her what it meant to stay and love someone without running away every time things got hard.

Maybe I was out of line saying that to her, but it was true. As far as I could tell, she was resorting to her old habits. She claims to have made these enormous sacrifices for the people she loved, yet she wouldn't tell me what they were. I'm sure she believed it to be true, but it's hard for me to believe, especially when I've been torturing myself with the memory of her walking away from me after that game all those years ago.

I climbed the stairs to my house and opened the door, not sure what I was going to do once I got in there other than pace the room worrying about Haley. But when I entered my living room, I found I had a visitor of my own. Thankfully, it wasn't Marcus, but my agent, Bo.

"Bo? What the hell are you doing in here?"

He grinned at me, "Well hello to you too, son. Your door was unlocked. Is that normal around here—do you think that's a good idea? I mean, you are a former NFL star. There are probably some eager, sticky fingers looking to lift some of your stuff, don't you think?"

I shook my head at him. "You didn't answer my question. What are you doing here?"

Bo rose from where he'd made himself comfortable on the couch. "Well, you kept dodging my calls and telling me it's complicated and you're not ready to interview for this commentating gig, so I thought I'd come out here and talk it out—get to the bottom of what's worrying you about it."

I shook my head. "Bo, I appreciate you making the effort and coming all the way out here, but it's not a good time. I just had this huge fight with Haley and..."

Bo looked confused. "Haley? The same chick from back in the day when you were in college?"

I glared at him. "If you're referring to the young woman I used to date, then yes."

Bo still looked confused, shook his head and muttered, "I thought I'd chased her away."

My head popped up sharply. "I'm sorry. What did you say?"

He laughed it off. "Nothing, just remembering something. No big deal. I didn't realize you two had reconnected."

I leveled him with a determined stare. "Bo, my knee may be messed up, but my hearing is not. What the hell did you mean when you said *I thought I chased her away?*"

Bo chuckled, "It was just a joke from a long time ago, poor timing as usual, you know me. I never know when to keep my big, fat mouth shut," he said before trying to change the subject. "Now about this job..."

"No, I want to hear more about this joke."

Bo heaved out a sigh. "Cooper, it's no big deal. You know, as an agent, when you're dealing with young impressionable guys, you have to grease the wheels for them to ensure everything goes as smoothly as possible. I was just referring to a time where I had to do that for you and frankly, I've had to do it recently too because let me tell you, it took some work to get this job lined up."

"Enough about the job. I'm not talking about the job. You chased Haley away... what did you do?"

"Cooper..."

"Bo," I ground out, "I'm not talking to you about anything else until you tell me what happened."

Bo looked like he deeply regretted his choice to come out to Hanalei, and that made me even more on edge.

I just had a fight with the love of my life and after proclaiming my love again, I insulted her beyond comprehension. Now my agent of over ten years looked like he was about to throw up, which indicated to me I was not going to like what he had to say.

Bo put his hands up defensively. "Look, I want to remind you that this was a long time ago. I would never do anything I thought might hurt you."

"Get to the damn point," I ground out.

He let out a long sigh. "I might have told Haley that it would be better for you if she weren't around."

I felt my face redden with anger, and it was enough to make Bo turn pale. "You were on a streak, and I knew you were going to kick ass in the league. But you were so enthralled with her. I was worried she would be a distraction, and that was the last thing you needed. So I might've told her that if she loved you, she wouldn't allow herself to be a distraction."

Everything in me stilled. I didn't know how to react to this. The anger was so intense. It had me in a chokehold. "And she listened to you, just like that? Walked away without a look back?"

Bo shrugged. "Well, no, to be fair, I had to wear her down. She was adamantly against it when I first suggested it, and kept giving me that young, starry-eyed girl jazz about how we can do anything if we're together, you know the story. But listen, I've been in this game for a long time and I've seen this cause promising players to crash and burn time and time again. So I stayed persistent, and you've had a wonderful career... you're welcome, by the way."

"Are you fucking kidding me?" I bit out. "You have the nerve to say you're welcome when you destroyed my life?"

"Don't you think you're being a little dramatic? Destroyed your life? I gave you your career. You are a star, my boy, and still would be if it weren't for that blasted knee. But hey, shit happens. You got eight good years in the league and that's a lot more than most people could dream of. Listen to me, when you want something that big, that magical, sacrifices have to be made."

There was that damn word again: sacrifice.

"That's exactly what you said to her, wasn't it? That she would have to sacrifice for the one she loves."

Bo decided to lean fully into this. "Well, yeah. It's true, and God bless her, she took one for the team. Listen, I know it couldn't have been easy. Young love always feels like it's going to last forever. But one little fight like you just had, or one bad day with Haley, could have upended your whole career. That's my job as an agent—to make those tough choices, especially when I have young recruits who don't have the life experience to make the right decision. I have to do it for them. It's not something I enjoy, son, it's just what needs to be done. You can't fault me for that. Look at everything you've achieved."

"I can and I will. What the hell is wrong with you?" I hollered, the rage bubbling up and pouring over now. I feared I wouldn't be able to control myself. "It's one thing to help someone with their career. But I never asked you to interfere with my love life. And not that it matters now, but Haley and I would've been just fine. She is the only reason I did as well as I did. She was my biggest cheerleader. Knowing she was out there, watching and supporting me, was the best I ever played. And even if I didn't, who cares? What does it matter? I got hit wrong one time and I'm out for life—with no Haley."

Bo was gesturing wildly, trying to hold on to one solid thread of his plan. "But you're not out for life, Cooper. That's why I came all the way out here. Listen, I know you won't be out there playing on the field anymore, and I hate that for you. If I could go back and undo that day you got hit, you have to know I would. But this deal as a commentator is the closest you're going to get to that field—and it's good money. Your face will be back out there. They will remember Cooper Barclay in all of his glory. You won't get that hiding on the island playing in the water all day."

I sucked in a deep breath through my nose and let it out through my mouth, trying to settle my anger. "I don't know how to get this through your thick skull. I love her more than anything—more than football, more than my name in lights, more than the money. And you took that away. You willfully pushed her away from me, and I have been in agony ever since. More agony than my fucked up knee or a career that ended too early. So whatever you think you did for me, this tough choice you had to make on my behalf, it's all bullshit, Bo, like this conversation, and like you coming down here. You're fired."

Bo's eyes flashed. "Now you listen to me, Cooper. You fire me, and this deal goes away."

"I couldn't care less about your stupid fucking deal. Get the hell out of my house, and Lord help you if I ever see you again."

Bo stood, smoothing his shaking hands over his shirt. "I know you're upset," he said, gathering up his bag. "I'm going to give you some time to cool off and then we can talk this out. We've been a team for far too long for it to end this way."

"I never want to see you again," I told him as he stood by the door.

Bo shook his head and then stormed out. It wasn't until then that I noticed how dark the sky had gotten.

The screen door slammed shut with extra force from the wind and as I looked through the window, I saw litter and debris flying through the air as neighbors frantically nailed pieces of plywood over their windows for protection. "Shit... Haley," I said, rushing out the door.

We'd weathered a few severe storms when we were kids, and had to help our parents get through, but I suspect it has been a long time since Haley had to deal with the wrath of Hanalei weather when it misbehaved.

I rushed over to her house, pounding on her door. "Haley! Haley, are you in there?" I called. I kept pounding with no answer and for once she'd locked the damn door.

"Shit," I cursed, punching the door.

"Cooper?" the neighbor from across the street called.

"Hey Mr. Landry, I'm just looking for Haley. I want to make sure she's all right through this," I called out.

"Oh, I saw her walking towards the Square about twenty minutes ago," he called back.

"Really? Thanks, Mr. Landry."

Why the hell was she walking to town when the sky looked like this? The wind was picking up speed by the second, and at any minute, the sky would open up and pour down on us.

As soon as I thought it, the first fat drops of rain began falling down. I barely had time to take a breath before those few drops turned into sheets of rain. Neighbors were hurrying inside their houses and some were still frantically trying to get boards up over the windows while I was headed in the opposite direction. I grabbed my poncho and started running in the rain towards the square. I had to find Haley and make sure she was safe.

I had to find her and explain everything—tell her I now understand the sacrifice she made, and that it never had to be. If it wasn't for Bo, she never would have left, and we would've been married by now with a house full of children. She never would have met Marcus, and I would've been the one to help her grieve her parents' deaths.

One selfish act by Bo has irrevocably changed two lives, but now that the truth was out, I was going to fix it. But first, I needed to find Haley and make sure she was safe.

HALEY

I would see to my parent's house as soon as I could, but my primary concern was the community center. I knew Cooper could storm proof his house, and I'm sure he was prepared. As worried as I was about him, I wasn't ready to face him yet.

So I concentrated all of my focus on the community center.

The place was rickety and falling apart. Now that I was teaching there several times a week, I was intimately familiar with its shortcomings and how one powerful gust of wind could be the end of the place. I'd spent some time exploring the property and knew there were storm supplies stored behind the center. There were plywood boards on the ready in case a storm hit, as they often did in Hanalei. I also knew where to find a hammer and nails.

I told myself I would rush over there, quickly board up the windows and then hustle back to my house to work on boarding up the windows there before hunkering down.

It had been a long time since I'd had to shelter in place for a storm, but it was coming back to me. The wind was whipping, but it felt like I had enough time to get to the community center and back home in time.

But when I was halfway to the square, the winds shifted and were so strong, I could practically lean into it. The sky went from dark to an eerie shade of light green and I knew I might have miscalculated, but it was too late to go back.

I tucked my chin to my chest, put my hands over my head to shield the rain, and ran as fast as I could to the community center.

I struggled against the wind to get the boards up and over the windows, but another resident came by to help me. I recognized him as one of the parents of the kids I taught. He didn't say anything, just jumped in to help me nail up the boards, and between the two of us, we made quick work of it. Before I could say thank you, he was running off to the next building to help.

Just then, the sky turned lighter, and I got a sinking feeling in my chest. Within seconds, big fat drops came down and then huge buckets of water poured from the sky in large torrents.

My house would have to wait and I prayed it wouldn't get too banged up, being so close to the water. I would have to wait it out at the community center until the worst of it passed and then get my butt home.

At first, I distracted myself by organizing the art supplies. The kids and adults alike usually did a pretty good job putting things away, but there was always an opportunity for a more organization. When the howling reached a fever pitch, and it felt like the whole building was shaking, I got nervous and squatted down in a corner. Now all I could do was wait for the storm to pass and hoped it blew by fast.

As I was squatting down in the corner, praying that everybody was okay, I worried about where Cooper was and I started thinking about everything we left unsaid.

We weren't guaranteed forever, just like Cooper and I didn't get our forever the first time. And we certainly weren't guaranteed a long time on this earth. My parents were proof of that. The only thing I was grateful for was the fact that they went together, which I know is what they would've wanted.

As I listened to Mother Nature take out her aggression on every building in Hanalei, I started making promises to myself if I got out of here unscathed.

First, I was considering leaving California. As much as I would hate leaving Tess, I'd already started rebuilding my life here, in Hanalei. It wasn't the craziest idea I've ever had. I was needed here—at least it felt that way—and this was the last place I had fun memories with my parents before everything got turned upside down.

I started thinking about the last time I spoke to them when I heard a loud crack and then felt water dripping on me from above. The corner of the roof ripped off like it was made of cardboard. Rain gushed in and I huddled further into the corner. As I tried to make myself smaller, my mind raced, and I vowed to do things differently from here on out.

I would tell Cooper I never stopped loving him, and the only reason I left was because his dumbass agent strong-armed me into believing I would mess up his career.

If I got out of here okay, I would come clean with Tess. She'd be upset with me, but she needed to know I loved her brother more than anything.

I would start being honest with the people who mattered most to me, including myself. No more running away—I had to face my feelings head on and learn to ask for help—and accept it without obligation.

The wind howled, thunder crashed, and I saw a streak of lightning through the hole in the roof as the rest of the roof threatened to rip off, flapping in the wind. "Please, please, please," I whispered to myself. "Please let me get out of this alive... please let Cooper be okay... please keep all the kids safe with their parents."

Another crash of thunder, and a loud roar that sounded strangely like somebody shouting "Hales!"

Cooper?

"Cooper!" I screamed, not sure if I really heard my name. But then the door burst open, and there was Cooper, sopping wet, his eyes searching wildly around the community center. I jumped up from my corner, rushing to him with my arms open. "Cooper!" I screamed, jumping into his waiting arms.

He squeezed me to him, holding me tightly as he kicked the door closed against the heavy winds.

"What were you thinking coming out here in this storm?" He asked as he cupped my face in his hands, his eyes roving over me to make sure I wasn't hurt.

"I wanted to get boards over the windows. I thought I had enough time..."

He shook his head. "You about gave me a heart attack. I was worried sick about you. There's more storm coming—so we're going to have to stay put for a while."

I nodded, tears of relief streaming down my face as I clung to him. "That's okay, because I have some things to tell you, Cooper."

"Okay, Haley, but first there's something I need to tell you. I owe you an apology. I've been really hard on you since you came back to town because of the way you left me all those years ago. But now I know the truth."

I looked at him in question. "When I got back to my place, Bo was waiting for me. He came here to persuade me to interview for this job he's lined up, but in the conversation, he let it slip about what he did to you—what he did to us."

I tore my eyes away from his, unable to see the pain there because it looked exactly like what I'd seen in the mirror for the last ten years. "Coop... I don't know what to say."

"Well, I do. I understand why you did what you did. But I want you to know this, Haley Ellis. I am not better without you. If anything, I am less of a man without you. The only distraction you pose is the good kind—and I want more of it, not less. I'm sorry he put you in that position. It breaks my heart to know I've been mad at you this whole time, when I should have blamed my greedy agent, who I fired, by the way."

I was openly sobbing now. Ten years. Ten years of agony, lost love and heartache. It was going to take more than a few apologies and tears to ease this pain, but this was a start, for sure.

"And Haley, listen to me. I may have been wrong about your intentions or why you left, but one thing has never changed—I've never stopped loving you. I know your life is complicated right now, so understand me when I say I'm not asking for anything from you. I just need you to know that I love you. That I have always loved you, and I will love you for the rest of my days. You get that right?"

I nodded vigorously, pulling him to me and kissing him, not caring that he was tasting my tears. We clung to one another, kissing the kisses of the heartbroken and long held wounds... ones that just might mend after all.

When we parted, I told him, "I love you too, Cooper, that never changed for me either. I think that's why I couldn't move on. Nothing felt right without you, so I kept making one disastrous decision after another... like getting engaged to Marcus."

A shadow crossed over his expression. "We don't need to talk about that now."

"No, we do. Cooper, the roof could be ripped off this place at any second, and I need you to hear this. I'm sorry I got so upset with you about Marcus. I've spent way too long doing what others think is right for me. And after I lost you, nothing seemed to matter anymore. So I didn't think it made a difference if I was in a passionless marriage. I figured I'd my chance and screwed it up, so I'd have to live with it. But I'm realizing now that my instincts were pretty good, even though I listened to others instead of myself. They led me to you—more than once," I smiled a watery smile at him.

He smiled back. "They sure did."

"This isn't going to be easy, Cooper."

He laughed, "I wouldn't have it any other way, Hales."

"No, I mean, I will not live in indecision and I'm not going to hide anymore. I love you and I'm proud of that... but that means I have to fess up to your sister."

He groaned and looked at me reluctantly. "That won't be easy, you're right, but it is necessary... especially if we're going to be together. I'm hoping that's what you want."

I grinned at him. "Of course, that's what I want, you big oaf," I said, mimicking Marcus.

Cooper laughed. "But we've been hiding this secret for ten years, so Tess may be mad at us for quite a while, and rightfully so. I need to know that you're in this with me and prepared for whatever her reaction is. I hate that our secret may cause a rift between you and your sister, but it's time she knows the truth."

He nodded solemnly. "Tess will be salty for a while, but she loves both of us, so I hope that love will bring her back to us."

We were silent for a moment, and then he looked at me hopefully. "You really mean it? You want to be with me?"

I laughed. "Cooper, I am in the middle of a hurricane and fearing for my life. There ain't nothing but truth coming out of this mouth right now," I laughed.

He pulled me to him and kissed me passionately just as the rest of the roof got snatched up. Cooper held me to him, murmuring soothing words in my ear, "It's okay, we're going to be okay. Let's move over here to the closet and try our best to stay out of the way."

"Cooper? Have you been in a storm this bad before?"

"Well, no," he admitted. "But we have to hold on a little while longer, Hales. Then you and I can get started all over again."

COOPER

B y some miracle, Haley and I made it through that storm... together. The town physician who was working his way building by building to check on residents found us in each other's arms.

After the roof was ripped off, there was no way I was going to let my girl go. I made sure she stuck to my side like glue. I already lost her once—I was never letting her go ever again.

Dr. Hammerstein had come to the island a few years before. He intended to retire here, but old habits die hard, and before we all knew it, he was opening up his own practice on Main Street. We were grateful he'd worked his way out to the community center to check on everybody along the way. The wind had died down, and it was eerily quiet when Dr. Hammerstein appeared where the door used to be and said, "Knock, knock."

We smiled cautiously. "Okay, let me look at you two and make sure you're okay. That was a hell of a spring shower we had, wasn't it?" He joked, but I could tell he was just saying that to cover his nerves. God knows what he'd already seen as he worked his way around town.

That storm was the worst one we've had in a very long time, and I dreaded to know what would meet our eyes once we left our safe little space.

Dr. Hammerstein looked both of us over and announced we were in the clear. "All things considered, you two are quite lucky."

"I wish I could say the same for the community center," Haley grieved.

Dr. Hammerstein nodded. "Yeah, it's a shame. But buildings can be rebuilt—it's a little harder to do that with people, so I am very glad you two found shelter here. Although Cooper," he said, pointing to the back of my hand, where there was a deep cut, "Clean that up as soon as you can to keep from getting infected. Stop by my office in a few days so I can check on it, okay?"

I nodded as he continued. "I can give you a steroid shot for that knee, too. I'm sure this weather hasn't been good for it."

I shook my head. "To tell you the truth, I hardly notice it."

Dr. Hammerstein smiled. "You will soon," he warned. "You two be safe out there. Come see me if you need anything," he made us promise, and we did.

That's when I looked at Haley, afraid to ask, "Well, you ready to go out there and see what's what?"

She shook her head. "No, this place is a disaster—the kid's mural is wrecked. What am I saying? The money from the festival was supposed to put a new roof on this place and now there's hardly a building to put a roof on," she cried.

I nodded, trying to calm her down. "I'm sorry, Hales. I know how fond you are of this place, but we both know that's the downside to living somewhere like Hanalei. For all its beauty, Mother Nature has her fits and we have to muddle through as best as we can. We'll figure it out, though, and find a way for you to still have your classes."

She nodded, but I could tell she wasn't convinced. I took her hand, and we stepped out of our devastated community center.

Dr. Hammerstein was right. My knee was killing me, but I couldn't worry about that right now. There was too much to be done, and as we made our way up to the town square, it was pure destruction.

"Oh, Cooper," Haley said in tears. "Look at all this. How are we ever going to get this put back together? Look at these buildings. They didn't get boards up in time and the windows are blown out."

We saw people cleaning up, looking exhausted and worried. We checked in with a few neighbors as we walked, promising to be back to help. It was going to take everybody in town to get this cleaned up.

The closer we got to our bungalows, the quieter Haley got, and I was worried. Especially when we saw that a couple of her windows were broken and water had gotten into the house.

"That's an easy enough fix," I reassured her. "We'll get everything dried out and cleaned up. I'll cover the broken windows with boards temporarily. There may be a bit of a delay to get you new windows, but we'll make sure you're tucked in safe and sound. And if it makes you more comfortable, you can come stay with me."

She sighed. "Oh, Coop, that's not what I'm worried about, although I appreciate it."

"What is it?"

"It's everybody else. It's such a mess out there. How are we going to rebuild this town? There's so much to do."

I put my hands on her shoulders. "I know it's daunting. But trust me when I say we are used to it around here, and if you're going to live here, you'll get used to it, too. But I also know you're my little list maker, so we'll get organized and help everybody get squared away, okay?"

"Okay," she said, and I could see she was already itemizing a list in her head of supplies we'd need to acquire.

I wish I could say my thoughts were that noble, but mostly, I was just thrilled she was right there beside me—and she was mine. I knew she and I could face anything together. But my immense relief took a hit when we both looked at our cell phones. There were messages from several hours before, most of which were from Tess. Text messages wanting to know where we were, if we were okay and telling us to get a hold of her ASAP.

I looked at Haley. "You know, if we just call or text her, it's not going to be enough."

Haley nodded. "FaceTime?"

So we huddled together in front of the screen and called Tess. I thought we were just letting her know we were both safe and unharmed. I didn't know this phone call was about to change everything for us.

I dialed Tess's number, and when her face popped up, her eyes widened. "Oh, thank God you're both there. This storm is all anyone is talking about and when you didn't pick up, I started freaking out. How is everybody?"

"A little worse for the wear. There's a lot of damage in town, but you know the drill. We'll clean it up, always do. Haley and I are both safe and sound," I assured her.

Tess leveled her gaze at me through the phone screen. "You're lying to me, Cooper."

I rolled my eyes. "Fine. I got a cut on my hand and my knee is killing me, but other than that, I am fine and so is Haley."

"I am so glad to see you two are safe. But while I have both of you, I got a strange call earlier."

"Let me guess, Marcus or one of his minions?" Haley asked.

Tess looked troubled. "No, it was Bo," she said, meeting my eyes, and a knot of dread formed in my stomach. "I thought it was odd when he called me and at first, I thought he was worried because he couldn't get ahold of you either, but then he kept going on and on about how I needed to talk some sense into my big brother."

"Over what?" Haley asked.

The worry lines in Tess's eyebrow deepened. "He said I needed to talk Cooper out of getting involved with you, Haley. He just rambled on about how it would be the end of Cooper's career and he thought he had nipped this in the bud, but he was going to need my help. Any idea what the hell he's talking about?"

I looked at Haley. I wasn't sure there was a way out of this. Tess was a smart cookie and she could see both of our faces. She'd know if we were lying. So when I looked at Haley, I hoped she would give me silent permission to tell Tess about our secret.

Haley looked at me, then at the phone screen. " Tess, he is referring to the fact that I'm in love with your brother... and I have been for a long time."

"I'm sorry what?" Tess said, shock written all over her face.

I saw Haley swallow hard. "It's something I should've told you a long time ago, Tess, and I'm sorry I kept it from you. We fell in love one summer when we were in college. We wanted to tell you, but then things didn't work out between us, so we figured it would be best to not say anything at all. No point in dredging up the past. But since I've been back in Hanalei, I've realized that I never stopped loving him and... we want to be together, Tess. We hope you can come to accept us and please know we love you very much. I know this is a lot to take in."

"You think?" Tess bit out sarcastically.

I saw Haley blinking back tears, so I jumped in. "Tess, I want you to know that I am all in, too. We understand you might be upset, but I don't want you to blame Haley. I'm as much at fault here. I love her, I've always loved her, and I don't see that changing anytime soon. But we love you too, and we hope you can be happy for us."

I squeezed Haley's hand, so proud of her for taking this step. This secret had been eating us alive for ten years and finally the weight toppled off our shoulders and it felt amazing.

That was until Tess's mouth snapped shut and her eyes strayed away from us, as if she was having to fix on a focal point other than us to keep her cool. I recognized that look. It was one she often employed when she was about to blow her lid.

Haley knew that look, too. I could tell by the way her hand squeezed mine even tighter.

I didn't realize I'd been holding my breath until it came out in a whoosh when Tess met our eyes on the screen, still silent.

"Tess, please say something," Haley pleaded.

Tess shook her head, her jaw set.

"How could you?"

Even though I expected this, the look of betrayal on Tess's face still felt like a punch to the gut.

"Tess," Cooper started, but she interrupted.

"No Cooper, this isn't the part where you big brother me and attempt to tell me why I should be okay with this. Sure, it's weird to think about you two together, but you could've given me the chance to wrap my head around it. Instead, you kept it from me for how long?"

Cooper and I were quiet.

Tess persisted. "No, seriously, when did this happen?"

I froze beneath her disapproving stare and Cooper admitted, "It was the summer before Haley was a sophomore in college, and I was a senior."

Tess shook her head in disbelief. "So this happened when I spent the summer abroad in Europe?"

"Yes," Cooper conceded.

"How long did this go on?" She asked. She was calm, but I could see the anger simmering in her eyes. "A few months," I admitted.

"I see," she said. "So let me get this straight. You two had a relationship behind my back ten years ago and it was serious enough that you both fell in love, but it never occurred to you to tell me."

"We were going to tell you, Tess, we just wanted to make sure it was the real deal first, but then we broke up so there didn't seem to be any point in making a big deal of it," Cooper explained.

"I see, so you kept your dirty little secret for ten years," she said, her voice rising with the last two words, and they felt like gunshots.

The betrayal in Tess's eyes was killing me, and I finally opened my mouth to speak. "Tess, please understand this is not something either of us is proud of. We thought it was in the past, but..." I paused, looking at Cooper. "Well, it turns out those feelings are still there."

"How nice. I am so freaking happy for you both, really," she said sarcastically. "How could you keep this from me? How is it possible it's never come up in conversation? You're my best friend. We talk about everything—this feels so evasive."

Cooper and I both shook our heads. "Tess, we know this is hard to wrap your head around, but I think with time..."

She put up her hand, interrupting her brother. "Don't give me that big brother schtick, Coop. I'm not in the mood. You're right about one thing... in time I would've gotten used to you being together, but I can't get used to the idea that you both lied to me. I mean, you're my big brother, my protector. And Haley, after everything we've been through together. I've had your back every step of the way, and you didn't respect me enough to tell me the truth," she said, fighting back tears. I could feel my own tears rolling down my cheeks as I tried to contain my emotions.

"Tess..."

"No. You know what? I can't do this with you two right now... I gotta go," and before either Cooper or I could say anything, she hung up the FaceTime call.

I stood there stunned with my mouth open as Cooper watched me carefully. "Haley?"

Cooper wanted to comfort me, but he didn't know how. So he took me into his arms and held me. I cried on his shoulder as rocked me back-and-forth in the middle of the living room.

I cried until I could barely keep my eyelids open. It had been such a long day...

Exhausted, Cooper and I broke apart and set about cleaning up the glass inside the house and putting a tarp up over the window. We left the rest of it for the morning. In the span of twenty-four hours, we survived a hurricane, officially reunited as a couple, and revealed a long-held betrayal to the person who meant most to us.

"Haley," he whispered, "it's time to go to bed."

I couldn't argue with him. I could barely see straight, and despite how tired my body was, I couldn't get my brain to shut down. "I don't know," I said, even as I let him lead me back to my bedroom. "I can't stop thinking about Tess and how to make this right. Then there's the community center and we need to check in on everybody again tomorrow to make sure they're all okay, " I rambled, as he plopped me down on the bed and helped me undress.

"There's so much to do," I continued, as Cooper tucked me in like a child.

"And it will get done, Hales, but first sleep," he said, pulling the covers first over me and then him. He snuggled up behind me and wrapped his arms tightly around me. I felt instant comfort and relief that he was back in my life for good this time.

"Coop?"

"Mm?" He hummed into my hair.

"This is not how I pictured getting you back," I admitted.

There was a soft chuckle in my ear as he said, "Oh Haley, I'll take you back any way I can—including weathering a big ass hurricane and a pissed off sister. I love you, and I'm never going to let you go again, you hear me?"

"I love you too, and I'm not going anywhere."

Soon, sleep would steal over both of us, and I was grateful.

I hoped that someday Tess would find a way to forgive us, but I had Cooper, and I was home.

Cooper

I fell asleep the night before with the warmth and comfort of the woman I had missed for far too long. But I woke up a few hours later to an empty bed. "Haley?" I asked to the early morning air.

I don't know what she could've been doing up that early. It was too early for me and I'm an early riser. But then I remembered—Haley was a worrier, and I feared it had gotten the better of her.

Sure enough, as I padded through the house, I could see her in the moonlight on the back porch, sitting on the loveseat with her knees tucked up under her chin, crying softly. It ripped at my heart.

I went out to the porch as if I was coming up on a scared animal. "Hales? What's going on? Talk to me," I said, taking the seat next to her.

She was staring at the now calm waters, shaking her head. "It's amazing," she said in a broken voice. "Those waves are so gentle and calming now, but think about how much destruction they caused just a few hours ago."

I nodded in agreement. "That's the thing about Mother Nature. She gives, but she also takes away."

"I hope everybody had someplace safe to sleep tonight. I should've checked before I got into bed," she said.

I reached out, running my hands through her tousled hair. "Haley, there's only one of you... and you can't help everybody all the time. Besides, you need to rest so you have the energy to help everyone."

"I just keep thinking..."

"That's your problem," I teased, and she glared at me through narrowed eyes, an expression I'd missed.

"Even if we do a fundraiser, it won't be enough to rebuild the community center, and we need funds—not just for that, but to replenish the slush fund to help the neighbors rebuild too. I've heard talk about the city having one, but I'm sure it's depleted after years of weather like this."

"Well, you're not wrong there," I confirmed. Hanalei did its best to maintain a rainy-day fund, but when you live on an island, storms frequently come through and the funds got used. It was difficult to replenish with so few residents—and even harder when we had a slow tourist season like we were having.

Events like the Aloha Festival were our bread and butter, but that often wasn't enough without additional tourist revenue.

"We'll figure something out, Haley, but it might not happen in one fell swoop."

She chewed on her lip now. "But what if it could?"

I eyed her curiously. "What's going on in that head of yours?"

She shook her head, clearly not ready to talk about it. "I'm not sure yet, but I might have an idea. It's going to be uncomfortable to execute," she said.

"But I figure I've done a lot of uncomfortable things lately... so maybe this is my big test. I thought it was admitting my feelings to you. Then I thought it was telling Tess everything. And those were hard things—but I also got the guy," she smiled, reaching out and brushing her fingers over my cheek. I turned my face into her palm, kissing it, and tickling it with the scruff I had yet to shave off after a couple of days.

Her expression sobered. "Tess hates me. I can't figure a way around that."

"She doesn't hate you—she just needs some time."

She looked back at the ocean. "I hate to disagree with you, but I can't think of anything that would smooth things over. There are no edible arrangements that say *'sorry for keeping a secret from you for a decade'*. If I'm being honest, I should have told her," she said, surprising me.

"What would've been the point? We weren't even together."

"Transparency? I mean, you need that with a best friend, right? All that time I told myself I had kept my mouth shut to spare her, but I'm realizing that wasn't it."

I looked at her in confusion. "What was it?"

She looked at me and tears fell unbidden down her cheeks. "It still hurt too much. It hurt to talk about you, it hurt to think about you, even though I did it all the time. I knew if I mentioned it, I would fall apart and I was never ready to talk about it. I kept waiting for a time when it didn't hurt so much that I could bring it up casually, but it never came. The pain always felt fresh. I know it couldn't have been that way for you, but..."

I scooted closer to her on the seat, then pulled her into my arms. "Don't make assumptions, Haley. There wasn't a day that went by where I didn't secretly wish you would come running back to me. All I could think about was yanking you back into my arms, and never letting you go again, if given a chance."

I buried my nose into her hair and inhaled deeply, finding instant relief in the familiar scent of her. "The only thing that gave me pause when you came back was the whole Marcus situation," I explained. "But I think deep down, I knew I wasn't going to be able to stay away for long... you're where I belong, Hales," I admitted, and she leaned her head back, looking at me with fresh tears in her eyes.

"That's how I feel about you—you're home," she said, and I couldn't help but kiss her. I tasted the tears on her lips, and we sat together on the porch for a long time kissing, getting to know each other again with no rush. There would be time for urgency later, but at this moment, my fingertips wanted to relearn all the dips and curves of Haley's face. My memories of her had to sustain me for over ten years. Now it was time to treat myself and discover all of her. We stayed out there for a long time, running our fingers over one another, familiarizing ourselves, and taking our time.

Finally, I couldn't take it anymore. I stood from the seat and reached down to scoop her up, carrying her in my arms back to her bedroom, and laid her out on the bed. We made love slowly, deliberately. I wanted to taste every inch of her, and even though my body demanded that I move more quickly, I was determined to savor every inch, relish in every little mewl and gasp.

When I sank myself deep inside her, she was nearly clawing at me. "Coop," she said, "Please, please."

I couldn't lie. The begging turned me on, but there was no way I could deny her. I started moving my hips with purpose. What started out as a slow lovemaking session turned into a frenzied coupling, needing to be consumed by her, to feel her kisses over my jaw as her small hands clutched onto my shoulders, reveling at her chants of, "More, I need more."

I knew with a certainty down in my soul that I would give this woman whatever she wanted. She wanted more. I'd give her more. If she wanted less, then I would give her less, although that would be difficult. She wanted me to take her to the moon—and I would make it happen.

After Haley and I reunited at the community center, I thought it might take a little time to let ten years of bitterness and resentment go. But in her arms, as we chased each other's pleasure, I felt that bitterness melting away, evaporating into the cool air that was coming in through the cracked window.

Could it really be this easy? Could I just let it all go and enjoy this woman forever?

I was ready to find out.

HALEY

When I woke up the next morning, I had a bone deep sense of what I was going to have to do.

Still, it rattled me. It felt like I was walking around somebody else's body as I pondered moving ahead with this idea.

The day before, I had felt, for the first time in my adult life, what it was like to be loved completely and without judgement. This wasn't the kind of love my parents had given me. Cooper didn't have to choose me, to love me. No matter how misguided, I ran away from him and stole years of happiness from us both. Now his sister, whom he adores, isn't speaking to us. No matter how we got here, I feel his love deep in my soul and I know this is it. I belong to him. I've always belonged to him.

I spent so many years dismissing my time with Cooper as immature, adolescent love, even as I struggled to move on. Then I made one relationship mistake after another, sabotaging myself, because I knew it could never compare to what I had with Cooper. Marcus had been the ultimate test. Could I move forward without Cooper? And the truth was when I saw him with Skylar, there was a thread of relief. And I unconsciously ran straight back to Cooper, right where I was supposed to be.

Even though it meant hurting my dearest friend, Tess. It was tearing me up inside, and I hoped we could fight our way through this. I understood why she was upset, and I would have to live with the consequences. All I could do now was hope for healing and forgiveness.

So I turned my attention to helping the community heal from the storm. After we made love, Cooper and I only slept for a couple of hours before we dragged our tired asses out of bed, got dressed, and wandered out to the street. We met several of our neighbors, out cleaning up their yards and repairing what they could. Thankfully, everyone had electricity and water, so Cooper and I did what we could to help them get settled before moving on to the community center.

Unfortunately, our beloved community center didn't survive the storm. When we arrived, there were already a dozen residents assessing the damage and beginning the cleanup effort.

There wasn't a lot of talking—people just handed out brooms to one another and shared trash bags. We took turns watching the neighbors' children while their parents tried to get a hold of the insurance company and schedule times to have their houses evaluated. Cooper set up an unofficial tag football game in the middle of the street to keep the kids occupied while I helped one of our friends clear out the spoiled food from her refrigerator.

"I appreciate you doing this, Haley," Mrs. Pepperdine said.

"It's no problem. Someday you may have to return the favor," I told her.

Her eyes lit up then. "Does that mean you're staying?"

I smiled, and she lowered her voice. "So you and Cooper..."

"It's funny how things like this bring people together," I beamed.

"You sound so casual, Haley. Like it wasn't fate, stepping in to make sure you two got back together," she said.

I sighed. "Yeah, well, I wish fate would have been a little less violent—then maybe we'd still have a community center. But I have a plan to build it back better than ever."

Mrs. Pepperdine patted me on the arm. "I'm delighted you're staying in Hanalei, sweetheart. You're a wonderful new addition to this community. I'm glad we get to keep you."

I reached out and gave her a hug. "I'm glad to be kept," I said, and I meant it. This wasn't just the rewriting of Cooper and my love story—it was about finding my way back to Hanalei—where I belong. I may have run away from my problems, but in the process, I found my people and I was so very grateful for that.

That's why I was willing to swallow my fear and put myself out there one last time, to make sure my people were taken care of.

While Cooper was distracted by the kids, I snuck back to my house for a few minutes to return a phone call I'd been avoiding for a long time.

My nerves made me feel a little nauseated as the phone rang in my ear, but I sucked in a deep breath, waiting patiently. This had to work.

Finally, a male voice sounded in my ear, "Clark Rivas, may I help you?"

I found my voice stuck in my throat for a moment, and Mr. Rivas prompted again, "Hello? Is anybody there?"

I cleared my throat. "Mr. Rivas, this is Haley Ellis, returning your call. I wanted to know if your offer still stands."

The conversation that took place was one I never imagined myself having in a million years, but by the time I hung up, I had agreed to a TV interview with the head journalist of the Celebrity Times.

I made it clear to Mr. Rivas that I he wasn't going to get anything salacious or scandalous, because that's not how I lived my life, that I wanted his questions to be clear and direct, and I would get to approve them before we sat down. To his credit, he promised we would stick to the script. I thought the entire process would take longer than it did, and I was both relieved and horrified when he said we could get it done today if I wanted to. When asked what he meant, he explained we could do the interview via videoconference. "That way, I don't have to book a flight to the island, and I can publish the interview as soon as possible. The sooner we do this, Miss Ellis, the quicker your check clears."

That was the part that relieved me. "While we're on the subject, Mr. Rivas, I'd like to discuss my fee. While you offered a very generous amount before, my needs have changed."

"You want more." He stated flatly.

I replied, "Yes."

To my surprise, he didn't balk. "Well, shoot me a number. What are you thinking, Miss Ellis?"

I sucked in a deep breath and said, "$250,000." That would not only cover rebuilding the community center, but it would replenish a healthy slush fund for the next storm and much needed to help our neighbors.

Mr. Rivas let out a whistle, "I have to admit Miss Ellis, for somebody who's so averse to being in the public eye, you're a savvy wheeler and dealer. I suppose you want me to keep that number under wraps, huh?"

I couldn't let him think I was doing this so I could pad my own pockets, so I told him about the recent hurricane and what happened to our little town.

"So let me get this straight. You're only doing this to fund repairs in the town you've been visiting?"

"That's correct, but I don't see what that has to do with..."

He chuckled. "No, Miss Ellis, I don't believe you do. Let me explain this to you from a journalist's perspective. You're the runaway bride whose ex-fiancé is a dickhead politician who's been talking trash about you for weeks. And while most people would want to defend themselves, you've kept quiet—until now and the only reason you're relenting to accept that big check for an interview is so you can help your neighbors. Miss Ellis, this story would have done well before, but now it's going to be fantastic and will sell itself. There's no way I'm not putting a spin on it."

I protested, but Mr. Rivas wasn't done. "Think about it this way... you will have an opportunity to showcase your little community, and we can put up a crowdfunding link for people can donate. So not only will you have the money from the interview, but you'll raise even more from people who resonate with your cause."

Surprisingly, Mr. Rivas was a willing partner, and even came up with a couple of other suggestions to raise even more funds. By the end of our conversation, my nerves had vanished, and I was excited.

Things moved quickly after that. Cooper and I had been up since dawn, so I had to do something about the dark circles beneath my eyes. I immediately phoned Evelyn and Natalie and they promised they would be over as soon as possible to assist.

I went into my closet to find something suitable to wear for the interview.

"Haley?" Cooper called from the front door.

"Back here," I called as I shuffled through my clothes.

He popped his head into the doorway. "Hey, where did you run off to?"

"I had some business I needed to take care of. I'm sorry I'm not out there helping, but I was trying to put something together that I think will help even more."

He looked at me confused and when I told him what I was about to do, there's a chance he would not be happy.

"Cooper, what if I told you I came up with a way to pay for the reconstruction of the community center and refill the town coffers times ten?"

He laughed. "What? Did you make a deal with the devil?"

His smile faded when I didn't laugh with him. "You could say that."

"Haley?"

"I agreed to do an interview, and it's happening this afternoon. I asked for more than they initially offered and they still accepted, so we'll have more than enough to cover everything that needs to be repaired."

"Hales," he said softly.

"I've already made up my mind, Cooper, so don't try to talk me out of it. Sure, I'm uncomfortable about putting all these details about myself out there, but it can't be any worse than what Marcus has already said about me. It's time to set the record straight—and I get to help Hanalei in the process. We'll get to rebuild the community center and continue to have a place to gather. It's a safe place for the kids to grow and learn—and I'll get to continue teaching art classes."

Cooper still looked concerned. "Okay," he said. "I can see you have your mind set on this, but please tell me you put some strict guardrails on how this interview was going to go?"

"Yes, I set my expectations with Mr. Rivas. He emailed me a copy of the questions he's going to ask with a promise he will not deviate. I know it's a gamble and he could go off script, but it's a chance I'm willing to take."

Cooper looked uncertain. "Hales, I am so proud of you for wanting to help like this, but this is giving a lot—maybe too much of yourself?"

I shook my head. "No Cooper, I'm done hiding."

He considered this, then asked, "Okay, what about Marcus? He's going to come back at you with a vengeance—are you prepared for that? I mean, I'm not going to let him get within fifty feet of you, though it would give me an excuse to dropkick his ass. But I'm just saying, I don't want you to have to deal with his retaliation."

I sighed. "Yeah, I've thought about that, and I'm ready for whatever he might dish out. It's not like I signed a non-disclosure agreement when I was with him, so I'm pretty much free to say whatever I want. But I'm not planning to go after him professionally, which is what he's afraid of, so as long as I make it about me, I should be fine. I'm sure Marcus will have a rebuttal and attempt to tear down my character, but everyone who knows me—the only opinions I really care about—will know he's full of shit. No one else matters."

He smiled. "Please, once everyone gets a look at you and hears what you have to say, they're going to be Team Haley all the way. I'm going to have to fight off a bunch of men with a stick, aren't I?" He teased.

I went to him then, dropping the hanger that had been in my hand onto the bed, and wrapped my arms around him. "I appreciate you being so supportive. I know you don't like it, but I really feel like this is what I need to do."

"And I will be here to support you. When's this happening, anyway?"

"This afternoon," I said to his chest as he held me.

He pulled back. "This afternoon?"

I shrugged. "Might as well get it over with. The sooner I do it, the quicker I get paid and then we rebuild Hanalei. Evelyn and Natalie are on their way to help me get ready."

"Okay, what can I do to help?"

I looked at him. "Can you be there? I don't need you in the frame or anything. I just need you to be nearby. You know, just in case..."

He smiled. "I wouldn't be anywhere else, my love," he said before leaning down and kissing me sweetly. "I love you, sweet girl, and I am so proud of you," he whispered into my ear.

"You have no idea how badly I needed to hear that," I told him.

Evelyn and Natalie arrived and miraculously helped me cover the dark circles under my eyes. They also helped me with my hair, so I looked somewhat presentable—at least the top half of me. I didn't look like a runway model, but I wouldn't scare any children who caught a glimpse of the screen, so that was a relief.

The interview time arrived, and I sat in front of my laptop, only after Evelyn repositioned it five million times to find my best light. The lighting was the least of my concerns. Thankfully, we got done with my hair and makeup with plenty of time to spare so I could review the interview questions one more time. I planned to answer them simply and keep to the point.

Once it was time for the interview, Evelyn and Natalie went out to the porch. They wanted to be supportive, but they didn't want me to feel more nervous with them watching, so they waved to me through the window with a thumbs-up sign. I was glad for my new friends, although right now I missed Tess. But Cooper was by my side, with an encouraging smile.

"No matter what, Hales, you got me," he reminded me.

I was so grateful for him. There was a very real possibility I was about to make a huge ass out of myself in front of millions of people. And once this was out there, I wouldn't be able to take it back. Being in large groups of people made me twitchy, so I was thankful this was a video interview and not in front of a live audience.

At the appointed time, Mr. Rivas appeared on my screen. "Miss Ellis, thank you for being on time. Are you ready?"

I let out of breath I hadn't realized I'd been holding. "As ready as I'm going to be," I said with a nervous smile.

"Alright, well, I have a producer behind me who's going to countdown, and after he says one, we'll be live. I'll introduce you and start asking questions. Don't think about people watching you Haley, it'll make you crazy.

You and I are just having a conversation like we did on the phone earlier. Let's keep it easy and stick to the points, alright?"

"Okay," I nodded, glancing over to Cooper, who gave me a thumbs up and a nod.

"Okay," a voice said behind Mr. Rivas. "We are live in three, two, one."

Mr. Rivas smiled broadly at the camera. "Welcome to Celebrity Times News. We have a hot interview that quite literally fell in my lap this morning and boy am I glad it did. You all have seen pictures of the runaway bride, leaving Congressman Marcus Tullane in the dust, but we've heard very little from the bride since her getaway. That all changed today. So, let me welcome Haley Ellis, the runaway bride. Haley, thank you for being here."

"Thank you. I appreciate the offer."

"Now Haley, I want to make it clear to our audience in full transparency, I have been trying to get an interview with you pretty much seconds after you ran out of that church," he laughed. "You've been resistant to giving any comment whatsoever. Can you tell me why that is?"

I sucked in a deep breath. "To be perfectly honest, I don't like being in the public eye, which sounds ironic now, considering I was engaged to a public figure. But also, I had a lot to sort through after running out on Marcus and needed some time to process what had happened and figure out where I want to go from here."

"That's understandable, and I'm glad you agreed to speak with us today. Now your ex-fiancé has been interviewed dozens of times, and each time he has smeared your name and reputation. Although you're not a celebrity like he is, you do have a reputation as a beloved art teacher at one of our local elementary schools here in San Diego. How does it feel knowing he has such awful things to say about you?"

I swallowed hard. I had prepared for this, so I knew what to say, but it didn't make the words come out any easier. "Well, part of me doesn't blame him, considering how I left him at the altar. He's hurt and embarrassed, so he's lashing out. However, Marcus is well aware of the events that transpired before the ceremony that led up to me leaving, so it's frustrating to listen to him lie, which only serves to make himself look better."

"Well, I'm not going to beat around the bush, so I'll just ask you outright what happened before the wedding that sent you running for the hills?"

I looked over at Cooper, concern etched all over his face. I nodded to let him know I was okay, then focused on Clark.

"I was having some second thoughts, which they say is common on your wedding day, and I was looking for some reassurance from my fiancé, so I sought Marcus out to have a conversation and..."

The words stuck in my throat. Once they left my mouth, I couldn't take them back, and there would be no containing Marcus's fury or hiding my embarrassment of that day.

"It's all right, Haley. Take your time," Clark encouraged.

I swallowed hard and looked into the camera. "Well, as I said, I was having some wedding day jitters, and I thought if I could just talk to Marcus, it would ease some of my worries. I went to the groom's suite and knocked as I entered the room—for future reference, I recommend waiting until you get a response before entering—and I caught him cheating on me."

"And that person was?" Clark prodded.

I told him before I wouldn't answer that question and I stuck to my guns. "I will not reveal the identity of that person. She was no one close to me, and I don't think it's fair to upend her life just because she has poor taste in men."

"But you think it's fair to oust Marcus?"

I bit my lip, measuring my words carefully. "That's different. Marcus is a public servant, and he has been openly lying about what happened between us. He knew what he was doing was wrong, and he did it anyway. When I caught him, he was more concerned with how it would appear to our guests if we didn't get married, than apologetic about what he'd done. He wanted to get married and work through his indiscretion afterwards."

Clark sucked in a dramatic breath. "He said that right after you caught him doing the dirty with somebody else? For some context, Haley, how long after you caught him did he say that?"

"I don't know, maybe five minutes."

"That's just wild. I can't imagine what was going through your head. So tell me, what happened next?"

I took another steadying breath, and glanced over at Cooper as a touchstone and then through the window at Evelyn and Natalie, who were doing silly dances to help me keep it light.

"Well, I'm not proud to say this, but I headed back to the bridal suite and got herded to the aisle by the wedding planner. Everything was moving so fast and before I knew it, I found myself at the end of the aisle with my maid of honor. As I was standing there, the reality of the situation hit me."

"Can you elaborate a little more on what occurred to you?" Clark asked.

"I realized it would've been a terrible mistake—even if I hadn't had caught him cheating. We weren't right for each other and I couldn't ignore it anymore. My timing was terrible, and I wished I would have dealt with it differently, but in that moment I panicked. I turned to my best friend, and told her I needed to get out of there and bless her heart, she had my back like she always does and she got me out of there and out of town, no questions asked."

"That's a good friend for you," Clark commented.

"The very best," I said, beginning to choke up. "I owe her a lot. Reporters and Marcus's representatives have hounded her ever since I left town, and she's doggedly protected my privacy during this time. She's a wonderful human being and I can't thank her enough. I owe her a lot."

"Well, considering all that happened, I'm glad you had her in your corner."

"Me too," I said with a smile, and I meant it. I hoped Tess would see this.

"So the last time I spoke to you off the record, you informed me you were staying on an island in Hawaii. We won't say where, for the sake of privacy, but it sounds like you've been doing okay since the scandal broke."

"It's been a journey," I laughed. "I know many people would think it was very convenient to head off to Hawaii after an ordeal like this, but my parents owned a small cottage that they left me when they passed away. I spent many summers here, and it holds wonderful memories for me, so it just seemed like the safest place to go. Coming here was the best decision I've ever made, aside from not marrying to Marcus."

"I've been able to reconnect with some old friends and make some new ones, and I've found my way back to myself. I don't think I could've done that if it wasn't for the people here," I said, holding back tears as I glanced at Cooper, who mouthed "I love you."

I bit back a watery smile.

"I am genuinely glad to hear things are turning around for you, Haley. Now, after the runaway bride incident, I assume Marcus tried to contact you. Am I to understand his attempts to persuade you otherwise didn't go so well?"

I shook my head. "No. They did not. I understand Marcus is upset and embarrassed, but given how things went down between us, I'm not sure why he was surprised when I didn't want to talk to him. He's very skilled at persuading others—a job hazard, I suppose—but when I wasn't buying it, he tried bullying me. When I didn't fold, he went to the press and dragged my name through the mud. Honestly, that part doesn't bother me too terribly much, but I teach young children and I worry they might hear some of that and actually believe it."

"That's right, you're an art teacher for an elementary school here in town and when we reached out for comment, we heard nothing but praise about you, Miss Ellis. So you heard it here first folks. She's not what the Congressman has painted her out to be—and I can confirm that for you based on my personal experience."

"Haley, there's one more thing I wanted to address with you. When someone's involved with a public figure, there's almost always more attention on them. That's something you've had to learn the hard way. As you said at the top of the interview, you don't enjoy being the center of attention, and yet here you are doing a televised interview for millions. You had a very special reason for agreeing to this interview. Full transparency for the audience, in case you didn't know, we pay all our interviewees. This was a hot story, so we put a big price tag on it and still Miss Ellis said no. But something developed over the last forty-eight hours. Do you want to tell us about it, Haley?"

"Yes, as most people know, tropical storms can be pretty brutal for the islands, and last night, our little piece of paradise survived a severe one. It devastated our community center and damaged dozens of homes. This isn't uncommon, and it's the price you pay for living somewhere so beautiful. But we're a small, tightknit community and it's going to be difficult to get enough funds together to rebuild the community center that is a vital piece of our community. This town has been so good to me and embraced me through this very difficult time. I have fallen in love with this place, and I want to see everybody here prosper and do well. It broke my heart to see the community center destroyed, but I knew with the right amount of money, we could build it back better than ever, as well as help our neighbors get their repairs taken care of." I explained.

"I was really touched when you told me why you finally accepted this opportunity for an interview. I genuinely got the feeling you didn't want to talk about your ex or your private business, but your community needed you and this was a way for you to take care of your people."

"This was too good of an opportunity to pass up and it could help so many people—that's all I wanted to do. All the proceeds from this interview will go towards rebuilding our community center and as many houses as we can. I'm also going to be auctioning off the wedding dress I ran off in, and we're hoping to use those funds as a slush fund for future storms because they are inevitable around here."

Clark smiled. "This is truly something to behold, folks. You took two dreadful situations, and you're turning it around. If that isn't the picture of civic duty and caring for your neighbor, I don't know what is. So listen up, we're going to be putting links in the show notes about where that auction is taking place and what you need to do to bid. We're also going to put up the link for a relief fund for the small town Haley is trying to help. She filled me in on some details, and there's a lot of damage. A few bucks from you, our audience, can really help. Haley, I want to thank you for taking the time to share your story, and we wish you the best as you help everybody get back on their feet down there."

"Thank you, Clark. I appreciate this opportunity and I appreciate you for hearing me out."

Clark signed off, and the screen went black. I snapped my laptop shut, letting out a huge sigh of relief, and slumped down on it.

"Oh, my God," Evelyn screamed, bursting through the door. "We watched the live feed, you were amazing girl," she sang out.

"Here, here, way to stick it to that rat, Haley, and what you're doing for Hanalei is nothing short of amazing." Natalie added. "I think we should bid on that wedding dress, Evelyn. If we win, we could frame it, and put it up in the diner as the famous runaway bride's dress."

"That's a fantastic idea," Evelyn said, smiling as she dug out her phone so she could look up the auction link. As those two put their heads together, Cooper came over to me with a warm smile on his face. "You okay?"

I nodded. "I just hope this works."

"Well, as long as the check clears, we'll have a new community center, that's for sure. I'm proud of you, Hales. I can't believe you did this for everybody."

I shook my head. "It's not all noble... I did it for me too, and not just because I wanted to stick it to Marcus—knowing him, he'll never really learn—but I love

this place. I love the people here, and I love the community center and getting to teach there. I want to fight for
the important things, and sometimes that means doing
hard things. "

Cooper took me into his arms and squeezed me tight.
As I gazed out the window, I could see my neighbors in
the street sweeping up. I pulled back, "All right, that's
done. Let's get back to work y'all," I said to everybody in
the room. I got back into a pair of shorts and my ratty
t-shirt, and we went back out to help clean up our town.

COOPER

I don't think I'll ever stop being amazed by this woman. She just did something incredibly scary and faced it head-on. I was in awe of her.

But I wasn't surprised. This was the woman who made the most painful decision of her life because she thought it was what would be best for me. That was Haley for you, always looking out for everybody else and putting herself last.

That's why I was worried when she agreed to do the interview. I thought it was history repeating itself, but the more she spoke, the more I realized she was doing this interview for herself. The love she has for Hanalei seems so obvious now, and she wanted to see us succeed. She would stop at nothing to make that happen.

So maybe it was time I took a cue from my girl and did some hard things too.

Firing Bo wasn't all that difficult when I learned of his betrayal. In fact, it's one of the easier things I've ever done.

But I would be lying if I said there wasn't a part of me that was intrigued by that deal. It wasn't a perfect fit, but the possibilities made me realize I wanted to get back to football. I missed it. And as much as I loved being on the island, sometimes I wondered if there was a way I could have both. I knew it wasn't likely, but I was going to face my fear and risk making a fool out of myself.

Shortly after Haley told me about the interview, I looked up the contact information on the contract Bo sent me months ago and I left a message with the network coordinators, telling them I wanted to talk and I had some questions.

I didn't expect to hear anything for a few days, so I was surprised when in the midst of helping one of my neighbors replace a window, my phone started ringing, and it was the network.

Haley was in the kitchen, helping the other neighbor clean up and organize what could be salvaged and throwing out what was trashed. I excused myself and took the call.

I wasn't sure if anything would come from this, but I had to try. "Mr. Barclay?"

"That's me."

The voice on the other line laughed. "Joe Jones here. I have to tell you I am tickled pink to actually be talking to you. I was still a junior reporter when I watched you debut against the 49ers—that was a magical game. I've been a huge fan of ever since."

I laughed. "Thanks man, I appreciate that."

"I am intrigued by your message. I'm also surprised to be hearing from you and not your agent."

"Yeah, well, Bo and I have parted ways. I understand that complicates things and you may not want to work with me anymore, but I have some questions about this deal. While I think it's a great opportunity, it's not the best fit for me now. I was wondering if there was a way to change it so it could work for everybody."

Joe was silent for a long moment before he said, "Well, it's a pretty standard deal as far as commentators go, but I'm interested in what you have in mind. What are you thinking, Mr. Barclay?"

I laid out my ideas and how I could benefit the network, but also told him that if it wasn't doable, it was fine. I was perfectly happy in Hanalei.

"Well, this is different from what we usually do. But I'll tell you what. Let me take it up the chain of command to see what we can do. I think you're worth fighting for Cooper, so let me see if I can sell this to my boss."

We said our goodbyes and hung up. I was excited, but I didn't want to get too ahead of myself. There was a real chance they would pass on this idea, so there was no point in getting my hopes up, but I was proud of myself for taking the leap.

Ever since I got hurt, I'd been hiding away in Hanalei, just like I accused Haley of. I shut down and become a hermit. The thought of being close to football, and not actually playing, has been so painful I couldn't entertain going back. But when Bo introduced the idea, I started getting excited again. That old adrenaline was coming back. I was wrapping my head around being part of things, just in a different way.

If I learned anything over the last several weeks with Haley, it's that not everything is what you expect it to be. I'd spent all this time being so angry with her, convinced she'd just heartlessly walked away. I never could have imagined what she'd really done was an act of love and concern for me. But now it was painfully obvious that I needed to be a little more flexible and open-minded.

I went back to work on the windows, and Haley and I were steadily working our way through the neighborhood, helping whoever needed it, when a booming voice sounded behind us from the street. "Where is Haley?" The voice sounded insistent. I popped my head out, blocking her from view because I didn't like the tone.

It was the mayor, with Mahina trailing behind him, a Cheshire grin on her face.

Haley popped up behind me. "Mayor? Is something wrong?"

The mayor grinned broadly. "Is something wrong? She asked if something's wrong. My dear girl, you have set everything right. Not only did I just watch your interview, but the phone lines are lighting up. We have more money in our treasury than the last twenty years combined. Not only can we build a new community center, but we can fix up some of the other city buildings and fast track all the improvement projects on the school. "

Haley's face lit up. "Really? That's awesome!"

I looked at her, astonished. "You did it, Haley. I'm so proud of you." I said, scooping her up into my arms and hugging her close to me.

"We don't do royalty here anymore," Mahina said, "but I think we just found ourselves a new queen." Everybody in the house laughed and gave hugs of congratulations to Haley.

The mayor looked at me in all seriousness. "I hope you're not dumb enough to let her go. "

I laughed, shaking my head, "Don't worry, Mayor, I may be a little slow, but I'm not that stupid anymore," I said, snatching Haley to me and giving her a long, hot kiss that had the adults in the room fanning themselves and the kids saying "*eww, gross.*"

Our cleanup after that was euphoric. The mayor was ecstatic about what Haley accomplished and told her, "You know what? With this extra money, we might be able to afford a part-time art teacher at the school—you wouldn't know of any teachers who might be interested, would you?"

Haley grinned at him. "Sign me up, Mayor. Besides, I'm staying either way, so you might as well give me something to do."

The mayor and Mahina hugged her sandwich style, and I was about to burst with pride. Unexpectedly, my phone started ringing. I hit the decline button, but it persisted.

I looked at the caller ID and saw it was Joe. Haley was distracted with the mayor and Mahina, so I ducked away and answered.

"Cooper?" Joe asked. "It's a go. My boss loves the idea. If you're in, we want you."

"Really?" I asked in disbelief. "That's amazing. Thank you."

"I'll have the legal department draw up your contract now. You should see it in your inbox in the next few days, so be on the lookout. Welcome to the team, Coop. We're delighted to have you."

I kept the news to myself until the end of the night, when Haley and I were strolling back to her house, hand in hand. "You seem awfully happy," she said.

"Why wouldn't I be? I have the prettiest, most badass girl holding my hand, and I'm about to take her home and do some wickedly naughty things to her," I said, winking.

She laughed. "Is that all?"

"Actually, I do have some news to share with you."

Her eyes widened. "Since you're in such a good mood, I'm going to assume it's not bad news."

I shook my head. "No, I think you'll like it. When Bo showed up, he was trying to get me to take a commentator job that would put me back in the game full-time. It's the closest I can get to football with my knee the way is. It was a good deal, but I didn't want to leave Hanalei and then when I fired him, it seemed like a moot point. But after watching you do something scary and brave, I decided I needed to do that for myself. So I called the network and pitched a new idea—I suggested being a part-time commentator, calling bowl games, but otherwise, I'd work remotely behind the scenes on content. I want to do more outreach too. They have a youth program in place, but it's only in big cities. So I'll work on expanding that too."

"That sounds like a perfect compromise. What did they say?"

I smiled at her. "They loved it. In a few days' time, I'll officially be a college football commentator and outreach specialist. I'll get to call a half a dozen games a year and when I'm not doing that, I'll be organizing their youth football camps across the country, including setting up new ones on the islands."

She stopped then and threw herself at me, and I laughed, twirling her around in a big hug. "I am so proud of you," she enthused. "It sounds perfect for you. You get to stay involved with the game, while also spreading your love of football with the kids."

I nodded. "Yeah, I'm pretty excited. I'll have to cut back on surf lessons, of course, but I'm alright with that," I laughed.

She beamed at me. "We're really doing this—we're putting our lives together."

"Together being the operative word, my dear Haley," I told her, kissing her softly on the nose.

She gazed up at me. "I cannot believe we found our way back to each other. I'm so very grateful."

I leaned down and kissed her sweetly. "No more grateful than me."

We walked arm and arm back to her house, and when we got there, we discovered several messages on the landline phone's answering machine.

Only a few people even had this phone number and they rarely left messages, but there were at least a half a dozen on there.

Haley looked at me, nervous, swallowing hard before she said, "Well, might as well get this over with," before she hit the play button.

A familiar voice rang in the air.

"Haley? Listen, I'm still really mad, okay? But... I also miss you. I think I'm going to be mad for a while, but I just wanted to hear your voice. I'll call back later." Beep.

Haley looked at me with hope in her eyes. "Tess," she whispered.

"I told you she'd soften up—in record time, too," I teased.

The tape advanced to the next message, and it was Tess again, although this time she didn't sound sad. Her voice was almost shrill as she shouted, "Oh, my God, girl, what did you just do? That was fucking awesome! Fuck that guy, I'm so excited for you!" Beep.

It advanced to the next message. "Haley! What. The. Fuck. I am so proud of you. I don't even know where to start. This is amazing. I'm still mad, by the way," Tess said before she continued, "but I'm also really happy for the two people I love the most. Listen, I can't get away for a couple more days, but I've already booked a flight. So I will come in personally to check on both of you pains in the asses. I love you..." Beep.

Haley looked at me with tears in her eyes. "It's okay, let them go," I told her, pulling her into my arms, and she soaked my shirt with her happy tears. I knew Tess would have to come around to my side eventually because she was my little sister, but there were a couple of moments where I was genuinely worried if she would ever forgive Haley.

I was so relieved for Haley's sake that she would be reunited with her best friend again—that loving each other wouldn't ruin her other most important relationship.

"You know what?" I asked Haley. "This has been one hell of a productive day. But there's still something very important we need to do," I told her in a husky voice, as I pulled back and led her to the bedroom.

She smiled. "What on earth could that be, Mr. Barclay?"

"Why don't you come back here and let me show yo u..." I teased.

She giggled. "Well, I will never tire of you showing me."

"Good, because I intend to do it for the rest of our lives," I told her as I pulled her into me, covering her mouth with mine, tasting home and forever.

EPILOGUE

*O*ne *year later...*

"Well, this is a vast improvement over the last wedding dress you had on, I have to say," Tess said as she smoothed out my short train to a loose beachy dress.

It was fitted at the bodice and then flowed around me in silky satin. Simple, clean lines, nothing gaudy. I had my hair down in soft beachy curls and light makeup, and this time, I had no reservations. I was about to marry the love of my life.

Cooper popped the question a few short weeks after the storm, and it was an easy decision. We waited all this time to be together, and we were tired of waiting. But we wanted our loved ones there, so we coordinated schedules and it came out roughly to a year after I had run away to Hanalei.

So much had changed in the last year. Mayor Khaled hired me as a part-time art teacher at the elementary school and I taught twice a week. The rest of my time was spent as the appointed Community Art Director, a title the mayor made up for me, out of gratitude for all the money I had brought in, and I was happy to take it. I loved spearheading projects year-round from the holiday market to the festivals, and I loved getting to know my neighbors through the process.

Cooper was a jet setter now. He spent a few weeks a year flying across the country calling bowl games, but the rest of his time was spent coordinating youth camps on the islands. He still coordinated other youth camps across the country, but he was able to hire staff to manage them in person so he could stay on the island. Occasionally, he'd visit the camps, and he was always so excited when he came home and told me about how much fun it was hanging out with the kids.

It made me look to the future. He was so good with kids. I knew in my heart he would be a fantastic father—but I wanted to have him to myself a bit longer.

Tess stayed mad... for all of four days. By the time she flew back to Hanalei for a visit, she ran to both of us with open arms.

We've been encouraging her to move to the island, and I almost had her convinced as we were preparing for the wedding, but she was still unsure about leaving everything behind in San Diego.

"I don't know. I like the hospital I work at and my coworkers, but my best friend is gone. Cooper is here. It does make sense," she said, relenting.

"So is that a yes?"

She looked at me through narrowed eyes. "Maybe. I need time to think about big decisions like this. Not everybody can run away on a moment's notice to the island and find the love of their life, Haley," she said, mocking me.

I laughed. "That may be true, but I sure am glad I could."

"I am too. You really are good for each other—even though you kept it from me," she replied. "But we're not going to focus on that... I'm excited I get to be your sister now. I always loved you like a sister, and now we'll officially be family."

I hugged her tightly.

"Haley," she said, in a strangled voice, "you're squeezing me too hard and squishing my corsage," she said, as I reluctantly let her go. She straightened her dress. I let her pick her own her bridesmaid dress, so I knew she was much happier with this little number than the hideous sack she'd worn for the disaster with Marcus.

When she got straightened up, she cocked her ear to the side, and we heard the first strands of music begin to play. She grinned at me. "Well, are you ready to walk down that aisle and make my brother the happiest man alive?"

I grinned at her. "Are you ready to give me away to him?"

This was one walk both Tess and I were looking forward to.

We walked down the makeshift aisle along the bumpy sand to Cooper. It only made sense to have the wedding on the beach. How could we have it anywhere else? The breeze was light, and the skies were clear.

The pastor started, "And who gives this woman away to be married?"

Tess beamed, "I do, her best friend, and now sister."

There was tittering in the audience as the pastor motioned for Cooper and me to step forward.

Cooper squeezed my hand, whispering, "You sure you don't want to run away?" He teased.

I looked him in the eye and said, "I'll never run away from you again, Cooper Barclay—you are mine forever."

THE END

Thank you for reading *Running Towards You*.

If you liked this book, then you will love *Second Chance with My Ex's Brother*!

Why you'll love it...

* One night stand
* Age gap
* Off limits/ex's brother
* Forced proximity
* Second chance
* Protective hero
* Wine country
* HEA

Here's a sneak peek...

One night. No promises. No last names. Just raw passion.
The twist? He's my ex's brother.
I slipped away at dawn... never knowing who he was.
Miles was my escape, a way to reclaim my fire and direction.
Our affair became a pivot point that altered my life's course forever.
Years later, I am the proud co-owner of a successful Sonoma winery...
And Miles is standing before me as a guest at the grand opening of my new resort—sexier than ever and still HOT

for me.

His kiss still sears and I want to give in, but I will not be distracted. Everything I've worked for hangs in the balance.

When the rest of his family arrives, the puzzle pieces come together, and I question everything—including his love for me.

Can I forgive his omission, or will our past extinguish the hope of a second chance?

Scan HERE to get your copy!

Sneak Peek
Second Chance with My Ex's Brother

One night. No promises. No last names. Just raw passion. The twist? He's my ex's brother.

I slipped away at dawn... never knowing who he was.

Miles was my escape, a way to reclaim my fire and direction.

Our affair became a pivot point that altered my life's course forever.

Years later, I am the proud co-owner of a successful Sonoma winery...

And Miles is standing before me as a guest at the grand opening of my new resort—sexier than ever and still HOT for me.

His kiss still sears and I want to give in, but I will not

be distracted. Everything I've worked for hangs in the balance.

When the rest of his family arrives, the puzzle pieces come together, and I question everything—including his love for me.

Can I forgive his omission, or will our past extinguish the hope of a second chance?

Scan HERE to get your copy!

PAIGE

"Paige? Paige, what happened?" Mia asked, running after me as I stormed into our apartment, tears streaming down my cheeks.

I tried to speak, but it came out garbled, even to my own ears. Miraculously, Mia did not need a translation. We'd been best friends since we were eight and sometimes, I was sure we could read one another's minds.

"That lying son of a bitch! You were always too good for him," she hissed in response to my tear laden explanation of my boyfriend of a few months unceremoniously dumping me. The man who I was certain was "the one" had casually ended things. When I had the audacity to be upset, he turned nasty, telling me if I hadn't been such a "cold fish" then maybe he would have stayed interested.

Mia sat back. "Maybe Leo needs a reminder of what a cold fish really is. I say we start by shoving a bunch of supermarket fish in his tailpipe."

"Mia..." I drew out her name in warning.

"Oh! Oh, I know... stick a few beneath his mattress and turn up the heat," she suggested, her eyes lit up. "You still have his spare key, right?"

I bit back a laugh. Mia was stone cold serious—and that's why I loved her.

"I saw that laugh," she said in mock outrage. "Laugh all you want, but I'll be adding a few pounds of scrod to my online order tonight," she promised before slipping away to the kitchen.

I listened as she rummaged around in the kitchen. I found one shred of calmness that allowed me to dry my face with the sodden tissue I didn't even remember plucking out of the tissue box.

How had I not seen this coming? Leo had been growing distant, but I'd chalked it up to his intense studying for finals. I still had a couple of semesters left before I graduated from college, but this was Leo's last semester. He was about to take the LSATs, and it would determine what law school he would attend. He came from a long line of lawyers: his grandfather, father, and older brother were all practicing. There was an expectation that everyone in the Townsend family would practice law and Leo had been tearing his hair out for weeks preparing for the test.

I'd helped him with flashcards, timed practice tests, and scheduled study breaks with homemade meals to ensure his success. We'd even planned an end of the semester party together in anticipation of him passing. It was going to be a big blowout for him and all of his law school bound buddies at his parents' lake house. Actually, Leo had secured the lake house while I hustled to plan the entire party because he was busy studying. Mia had warned me I was doing too much. "You have your own finals to study for," she'd reminded me.

To which I replied, "I know, but this is an important night for us—one we will remember for the rest of our lives."

Soon after, when he'd met me after work to give me the good news that he'd passed the LSAT with flying colors, I launched myself at him with a congratulatory hug. I didn't understand the uneasy look in his eyes when he'd set me down away from him and told me we were over.

"I mean, really, fuck that guy. After everything you've helped him with. Not to mention you put all of your plans on hold for him. You even changed career paths because of him," Mia fumed from the kitchen as I stared at the wall. Sadly, she was right.

I wanted to get my degree in business. Running my own business sounded like fun. I hadn't been sure what kind of business that would be until shortly before Leo and I had gotten involved. I recently started working at a fancy restaurant on the opposite side of town. Not only were the tips great, but I no longer left work smelling like a greasy spoon like I had at my previous serving job. The restaurant, Bella Nova, took its menu seriously. So much so that the waitstaff was required to take a wine education course so we could recommend proper pairings with the dishes. I'd only just turned twenty-one when I took the job, so I knew nothing about wine. But in the last few months, I'd become intrigued and a little obsessed with the extensive process that went into creating an excellent wine.

When I mentioned my dream of opening a winery someday to Leo, he laughed. "You're telling me you're going to spend all your time learning about alcohol?"

"Well, yeah. It's a multi-million-dollar business if you can create a place for yourself. And I'm enjoying all the stuff I'm learning." I explained.

He smirked at me. I should've read that as a red flag and then he said, "sounds to me like you want to be a professional wino." I had taken it as a joke instead of the insult it was.

Leo was smart, and he held himself with such confidence that I never questioned him. Somewhere along the way, I'd lost myself and got swept up in the idea of being in a relationship and being loved.

I was so focused on being what I thought Leo wanted that I had let him talk me into changing my major. He convinced me I should work at his law firm with him—not as a lawyer, of course, because he wouldn't want to compete against his girlfriend. But he said they always needed mediators. I hadn't completely understood what the job entailed, but when he described to me, it sounded boring as hell. He sold it as something respectable and stable, so I had agreed. I had been fighting my way through the classes, trying not to fall asleep—all for nothing.

"This sucks," I said, from my place on the couch to Mia. "I mean, I met his whole family—well, most of his family. I never met his older half-brother. But I sent him a video message."

"You sent him a video message?" Mia asked, confused.

"Yeah, one time when I was at his parent's house, Leo's mom was worried because I guess his older brother had been having a hard time. So, she was going around recording everyone giving encouraging words to Wallace. But Leo couldn't be bothered, so she asked me to give him some encouraging words instead. I hadn't even met the guy, but she seemed happy with it."

"I bet his mom's going to be heartbroken over this one," Mia said.

"I know. I'm going to miss her. She was really nice. She made me feel like—like I was a part of the family."

Mia laughed. "I'm sure she wanted you to be part of the family... I don't know any mom her age, with a son, who doesn't look at you and think daughter-in-law material."

I swallowed around the fresh lump of emotion growing in my throat. Yet another thing that sucked about this whole situation. Even though Leo and I had only been together for a few months, things moved quickly. I had already gotten to know his parents, and I was supposed to meet his half-brother Wallace at graduation. That wouldn't be happening now. I'd spent the last few months thinking I was marching towards my happily ever after, and he snatched it away just like that.

Mia returned, this time with two steaming mugs of tea. I looked down at the murky liquid. "Don't worry, I put a little whiskey in there," she winked.

I smiled at her.

"It may not seem like it now, Paige, but you're better off without him. Somewhere out there is your knight in shining armor. I know it," she assured me.

"I wasn't looking for a knight in shining armor... I was hoping for a nice guy who would love me for me."

She nodded. "Well, Leo isn't that guy. But the right one is out there and we're young, so there's no rush."

I nodded in agreement. "You're right, as usual." I was feeling a little better after her pep talk when a text message alert on my phone chimed. I lunged for it, thinking it might be Leo and I was right. The words that met my eyes were not flowery words of regret and professed love. Instead, they read:

Hey, I know what went down between us is still a little raw, but would you mind getting a hold of the DJ for the party and asking him to be here an hour earlier?

I let out an angry sigh.

"Oh no, what does it say?"

I handed Mia the phone and watched her eyes nearly pop out of her head as she read the text. "The nerve of that asshole. I mean, he stomped on your heart and now he's worried about this stupid party."

"Yep. A party I drove myself to distraction over planning. Nit-picking every single detail instead of studying more for my finals," I fumed.

Mia looked at me for a moment, and then a wicked grin spread across her mouth. "The party you and I are going to crash," she said.

I sat up from the couch. "Oh, no, how humiliating would that be?"

"Not at all, and I'll tell you why. You're going to put on your sexiest dress and strut into that party like you own the place. He's going to realize how bad he fucked up, while you and I have a grand old-time dancing with cute guys."

I shook my head, recoiling at the thought of what she was suggesting.

"Come on, Paige," she pleaded. "I understand you're hurt, I do, but do you want to shrink away that easily? This guy needs to understand he can't behave that way. If he wanted to end the relationship, fine, but he could've had some compassion."

"You won't get any argument for me," I agreed.

"Think about it Paige, think about all the things you have changed and sacrificed for this guy. It's time to take it back."

As I plopped back down on the couch, a fresh wave of mortification rolling over me when I thought about all the changes I made to be a "better fit" for him. I had changed my major, my career path, and a hundred other little things to make him happy. Somewhere in all of that, I lost myself. I never used to twist myself into a pretzel to make somebody happy, but in my quest for love and companionship, I had turned into a complete doormat.

I'd watched my mother cater to my father's every whim. It was in those rare moments when we were alone that I experienced how vivacious and fiery she was. I remember being flabbergasted she wasn't naturally this mousy, subservient woman. But after so many years with my father, she had folded herself into what she thought was a much more palatable version of herself, at least for him.

It made me resent him and his bullishness, and I had wondered why she had stayed with him. By the time I left for college, I had accepted that people stayed in relationships for their own reasons and it was between the two of them. She was an adult, and as much as it broke my heart to watch her hide her sassy side, I knew I had to continue to be the force of nature she raised me to be. For both of us. Then I met Leo...

It's not like he asked me to change everything about myself. I just followed the example I was shown my whole life.

"Wait a minute, what's going on here?" Mia said, waving her hand in front of my face. I pulled myself out of my contemplation and looked at her with determined eyes.

"I had a major epiphany," I said, feeling the strongest I had in a long time.

"Oh? Tell me," Mia said with raised eyebrows.

I took a deep breath before I admitted, "I think I was just mimicking my parent's relationship. Without realizing it, I was following in my mother's footsteps."

Mia looked at me, then added, "I believe that's what Oprah would call a lightbulb moment?"

I laughed. "Something like that, but I think you're right. I planned the damn party. Why shouldn't I enjoy it?"

Mia clapped her hands together. "All right! That's my girl! Now, we need to go shopping for some new outfits. Operation: Make the Boys Sweat is underway," she said in a singsong voice as she floated to her bedroom.

I had a smile on my face even as uncertainty settled at the bottom of my stomach. If I was going to stop being the doormat I've become over the last few months, then I was going to have to make some big changes, no matter how uncomfortable they were. I already had a long list in my head of everything I needed to do to reclaim my life. But first, I needed to show up at that party and show Leo exactly what he was giving up.

"I don't think this is such a good idea anymore," I whined as we neared the lake house.

Mia looked over at me sharply. "I love you, but if you say that one more time, I'm going to have to give you a sisterly slap."

"You would really do that?"

"If it's what it takes to snap you out of this, then yes. It's all out of love, of course," she said.

I rolled my eyes and shook my head. "I'm getting more anxious the closer we get to the lake house. This will be the first time I have seen him since he dumped me, and I feel like such a loser."

"But you're not a loser and don't get in your head about this. Come on, you are dressed to the nines and you look sex-eee," she said, drawing out the last word. "I look pretty good too," she said.

I laughed. "We both look pretty good," I admitted.

"We are stunning, but what's going to make us go from looking good to knock out is how we walk into that party. So, tell me again," she insisted, wanting me to go over the plan for the hundredth time. It was getting annoying, but I couldn't blame her, considering how nervous I was.

I sucked in a long breath, then recited, "We go in head held high, hips swaying, and we talk to everyone but Leo."

"Exactly!" she said with a decisive head nod. "And, if you can find yourself a stud muffin and start chatting him up, that would be icing on the cake."

I laughed. "I don't know. I know most of Leo's friends. Some are cute, but I'm not sure any of them qualify as a stud muffin... where did that term come from, anyway? Your Grandmother?"

"Hey, Granny has some pearls of wisdom, so what if her terms are a little outdated?" she countered.

I relaxed and focused on Mia's words as we approached the lake house.

I'd been out here once before with Leo's parents, and it was beautiful. It was empty most of the time, and I knew his parents were thinking about turning it into a vacation rental for tourists. I'd had fun decorating the place for the party. There were several times in the last three weeks since I'd been in and out of the house setting up that I stopped to watch the sunset over the lake.

Although the house was a little big for my personal taste, it had a stunning view. When I looked out of the big plate-glass window in the living room towards the backyard, I spied a pier that stretched over the edge of the lake and led to a guesthouse. I hadn't seen the inside, but it looked like the perfect place to escape for a little while.

I knew that if I got overwhelmed during the party, I could look out the window and escape to the guesthouse on the water. I had even revealed this plan to Mia, who replied, "Don't you be escaping to that guesthouse. You need to stay present and hot—that is our mission."

When I looked a little terrified at the thought, she reminded me, "My phone is on me—the second you need to go, just text me and we will get the hell out of there."

I remembered that promise now and took comfort in it. I was so lucky to have her as my best friend. There is no way I'd survive this without her.

I rubbed my sweaty palms over my thighs, tugging at the short hem of my dress. It was a sexy little sundress that hit mid-thigh, with spaghetti straps over a peasant bodice with a little keyhole tie at the front, revealing an ample amount of cleavage. This is the most risqué dress I've ever owned, and it made me self-conscious. When I slipped it on in the store, Mia had assured me this was the dress that would make Leo eat his heart out. I paired it with some strappy sandals and swept my hair back into a French roll with loose curls framing my face. I felt overdressed for a causal lake house party—but we were going for sexy, and Mia assured me it was.

Every time I shifted in the car seat, I felt my boobs slip further out of my dress, and it was a little nerve-racking knowing I was revealing so much. When Leo and I had been together, I dressed more conservatively. This memory irritated me and made me stick out my chest a little more.

It was time to get the old Paige back and she never would have given a shit about how revealing this outfit was.

Mia found a place to park, and I took a deep breath before I stepped out of the car. She rushed around the front to grab my hand. "Remember who you are. You are Paige-fucking-Russell, a woman not to be messed with," she said in my ear as we walked into the party.

The place was already bustling, and the drinks were flowing. I noticed Leo had added a keg, which I had argued against when I planned the party, but I knew there would be a couple of bottles of wine in his parents' wine cabinet. I would find my way over there at some point. In the meantime, I girded my loins against the onslaught of rowdy partiers.

"Dammit, I should not have had that big ass soda before we got here," Mia said, squirming next to me.

"There's a bathroom down the hall to the left," I said, pointing toward the restroom.

She looked at me with uncertainty. "I do not want to leave you here alone."

I patted her on the shoulder. "I'm a big girl. Paige-fuck-ing-Russell, remember? I'll be okay. Find me when you're done."

She gave me a grateful look and leaned in to say, "Nine o'clock. One of those stud muffins is checking you out. You can thank me later," she winked, rushing off to the bathroom.

My gaze went in the direction she had pointed and met a pair of intense, dark eyes that were watching me.

I felt the blush crawl down my body along with the man's eyes. He was tall, broad-shouldered, and shame-less, by the way he was looking at me.

I swallowed around the nervous lump in my throat. I've never had a man look at me like that before. He looked unfamiliar to me—and older than everybody else here. I wondered who he was, as I turned to walk away.

I wandered through the house greeting people I rec-ognized and congratulating the ones who were still sober enough to understand what I was saying.

As I slowly made my way to the wine cabinet off the side of the kitchen, I heard a playful giggling and a fa-miliar voice.

I stopped in my tracks, following the sounds. It was coming from Leo's father's office. The door was ajar, and when I looked inside, I glimpsed an ass I recognized all too well—Leo's.

My eyes traveled upward, and I saw his ass drilling into a beautiful girl I recognized from one of his study groups. Her head was thrown back and her hands clutched his shoulders as he fucked her over the desk.

Everything inside of me went cold. Did they even realize the door was open, or did they just not care?

I sucked in a breath and got my feet to move, rushing away from the scene of the crime. Except it wasn't a crime, was it? Leo and I broke up. What he does now is none of my business.

I made it to the wine cabinet and selected my vintage of choice with a decisive flourish. I poured myself a generous glass, took a large sip and tried to erase the image replaying in my mind.

Leo had always wanted me to do something wild like that, but I didn't want to disrespect his parents' home, especially if I was going to be a part of the family.

We'd had plenty of sex, but we could never be too boisterous. There was always a roommate on the other side of the wall or his family down the hall.

He was always grooming me to be a lady—to conduct myself as someone who could be a future lawyer's wife. I had to be put together at all times. I guess now I understand what he meant when he called me a "cold fish." He wanted someone to bend over his father's desk. I didn't hate the idea, though now I hated the idea of it with him.

I looked up from behind the kitchen island and, once again, my mystery man's eyes were on me. He was much closer now, though still a respectable distance away. He was close enough now that I could tell they were dark brown... and they were looking at me like I was naked.

Emboldened by heartbreak and anger, I held his gaze as I brought my wineglass to my mouth again and took a healthy swallow. One side of his mouth quirked up, bringing my attention to his full lips. He had some stubble on his face, and suddenly I wondered what his stubble would feel like against my skin.

"Paige," a whisper came next to me, and I nearly jumped out of my skin. Mia was next to me now, and teased, "I see you and stud muffin have progressed to eye fucking. I have to say I'm proud of you."

Scan HERE to get your copy!